The Rasumovsky Quartets

Love, Music, Politics

A Novel

By Mark Paffard

ISBN: 9781797408101

CONTENTS

Wilt thou enjoy the pleasures of love with purest of feelings?

Keep conceit from thy heart – banish solemnity!

Love is scared by the one, the other hopes vainly to chain him:

Ill-affected to both smiles the mischievous god.

Goethe, epigrams XV

The Narrators – Rasumovsky's String Quartet

Ignaz Schuppanzigh – 1st violin

Josef Mayseder – 2nd violin

Franz Weiss – viola

Josef Linke – cello

First Quartet: 1809-10

1. Linke (20th-22nd May 1809)

Prelude-1806
'Beethoven drinks too much.'
' - He must be drunk, to write such stuff!'
'Yes. Maybe. All the same, this…'
(A passage was heard on the viola.)
'Quiet,' I said, 'here he comes!'

It was, indeed, the composer. We hastily closed our scores - Weiss, the viola, last - for though the scores had been already laid out before we came, it was too much like being caught, to have looked at them at all *before* we played from sight. We *were* a little afraid, reluctantly, of Beethoven. Like a bunch of schoolboys we had endured his temper before, and even our leader, Schuppanzigh, who had known him for years, looked at him with a wary eye.

I, for one, was fearful, then, of the Rasumovsky palace – and of Count Rasumovsky, the Russian Ambassador. After all, there were only Russia, France, and music left. And England, but where was England? The French had already made whores of the Viennese. To be an Austrian now meant nothing. I even looked forward to going home again – back to dull simple Breslau, in Silesia, even though it had never been much of a home.

On and on Beethoven came, like a little storm-cloud, travelling under the gilt-edged sky of the ballroom; and at once, from another direction, there came the measured tread of Count Andrei Rasumovsky. With him was a very old man: clearly another aristocrat by the elegant cut of his clothes, which, however, were slightly shabby and hung too loosely upon him. He took a seat some distance off where he remained throughout. We all stood up and bowed. Our host waved us genially back to our seats; but as he turned to bow, once again, to Beethoven, he was disturbed by a third entry – a clumping and a sibilant rattle, like some discordant timpani. We all looked up in alarm, but it was only Madame Sophie, Weiss's club-footed wife, bringing in a tray of crystal glasses, and

1

champagne. The Count had found a room for me in the palace, and for Franz Weiss and his wife, a cottage out in his palace gardens. We could see it through the French windows from where we sat. Since these three quartets, written for the Count, were still in the nature of a secret (one to be kept, that is, from other wealthy patrons), it was natural that Sophie, not one of the usual servants, should bring us our champagne.

That day we were trying out the first quartet, the others being incomplete. Rasumovsky took Mayseder's violin. That young man stood aside, looking rather sulky. One could smile – one was meant to smile – at the fact that the Count had *not* brought his own Stradivarius. Mayseder's scuffed little instrument looked so very incongruous in his hands. He played it well enough, more or less keeping pace. Only to my mind his playing, even at sight, did somehow *appropriate* the music, even though he was clearly as puzzled as the rest of us. Beethoven didn't seem to mind. Perhaps he held no great expectation, or his mind was occupied elsewhere, with his new symphony.

I had the melody, a swift dark stream of a tune over which, it seemed to me, the others passed like flashes of light.

'How was it?' asked Rasumovsky, wiping his brow. He speaks a fluent, emphatic German.

'Fine,' said Beethoven tersely. 'Not too sweet,' he added, and turned his back. In those days his hearing was only slightly impaired.

The Count frowned and nodded in diplomatic style. He waved Mayseder back to his place for the second movement. We played on without a hitch, and I began to hear the other parts, as I relaxed and the thing uncurled itself – scherzando, adagio, and swift, brusque allegro. It was in those final bars that the other thing happened. The Count was standing by Sophie. Perhaps he jogged her elbow. There was a crash, a cry, a shattering of crystal, the clump of a boot, a growl, and then a stifled laugh - but we could no more stop playing than cavalry on the charge until, with almost a flourish, we hit the final chord.

The bottle of champagne lay guillotined in a pool of froth; the crystal glasses completely shattered, save for just one that the Count had evidently caught in its fall. He knelt in the wreckage, below the pallid Sophie, and waved her back with a hand from which blood dripped freely. Then he gazed up, bewildered, into her face. He was no longer the jovial, long-nosed bear, whose dancing, we had heard, made all the ladies quiver. Nor was he the ever-composed, austere, semi-Viennese lord, brother-in-law to Prince Lichnowsky (though recently and suddenly widowed.)

After what seemed a long age, Sophie asked:

'Sire, should I fetch more wine?'

He looked up at her, and then at us. Then he nodded gravely:

'If you would be so kind.'

As we drank to the first new 'Rasumovsky' quartet, we all knew that something strange had happened; but none of us guessed that this would be the start of a long, and passionate, love-affair.

***

May 20th, 1809

It is three years on, and hot summer. In the interim Weiss and I have both returned home to Breslau, save for a few months every year in the winter music season; winter months that Count Rasumovsky has employed in seducing Madame Weiss – except that seduction is not the right word, for still neither he nor she seem to know what they are about. But now that those quartets are published - as Opus 59 - the Count has decided to have his own private string quartet, and so Weiss and Sophie have come to live in that same cottage, making the palace their home.

Meanwhile the French, who were here in 1805, just before Austerlitz, and then in Breslau in 1806, blasting it to rubble, have once more, with a few cannon shots, taken Vienna from the lazy Viennese. They have taken over the city and quartered themselves on the burghers, but they have yet to meet with the Austrian army, which is manoeuvring somewhere across the Danube. There is to be yet another great battle, and we are in the thick of it. Life goes on, but as the heat rises the tension rises too.

My older brother Johann died at Austerlitz, where he was loading cannon. I suppose he is buried somewhere, mixed up with the Austrian dead, and those Russians who did not escape with their useless general Kutuzov. My father (a butcher) and my mother both managed to die of the plague, so we were brought up by Holy Fathers who taught us and beat us in equal measure, until, unfit to be priests, we were turned out to fend for ourselves; though I shall always be grateful to father Gregor, who taught me the cello. In Breslau I first met Weiss, whose father, a Protestant pastor, died in that same bombardment.

Johann married for love, but found it hard to make a living. He worked as a coachman, a builder, and on his in-laws' farm, which latter drove him to enlist for the war. His widow, Anna, and his daughter, Therese, were left with Anna's parents - peasants tied to the royal estates south of Breslau, selling their meat and living as best they could. In harvest time I would go and help, stumping the dusty fields with my foot; for, strange to say, I have the same affliction as Sophie. But when I found work in Vienna in 1806 I took them away from the farm, where they got blows and little to eat; and now that I am appointed cello in Count Rasumovsky's quartet I have brought them here for good, to where the skies are raining gold. They are in my own apartment, I am in the Count's new palace, and the French Army are in the streets.

In the Count's library we rehearse for our first public performance: though, with so many nobles absent because of the French, one wonders when it may be. We are taking on the Quintern quartet of Haydn, Mozart's twenty-first (which old Prince Lichnowsky claims to have seen him write in Potsdam), and that same quartet of Beethoven, first of the Opus 59. Our leader is Ignaz Schuppanzigh, a Viennese of the Viennese; a bottomless well of music and fatter than a hog; a prince who commanded us hither to be in this quartet, and a jester with his bow. Now he drives us hard, moulding us to his vision – and then declares that there are many ways to skin a cat. He puts his hand on his half-female pap and calls out: 'Not too sweet!'

'Who was that man?' Mayseder asks me as we are packing up.

'The one in the black coat? His name is Peter Andreyich, the uncle of our Count. They say he is very fond him. He has his rooms right here –'

I point across the hall to the suite of Rasumovsky's former wife. Between these and an empty storeroom where the flue goes up from the kitchens, just opposite the library, I have a room for my own use: a small, unnoticed room with a window of milky glass, and, in the centre, one blue panel showing Noah's dove.

Mayseder shudders: 'He is odd.'

'He seems to like Beethoven's music. Are you going round to the Schwan?'

'Are you, Josef?'

I hesitate. It is always an event to see Beethoven, but he is certainly not at his best in a crowd. Nor can one be sure that the Schwan, his favourite tavern, will not also be occupied by French troops.

It strikes me that I will go to Anna and my niece, Therese. I am teaching the girl the fiddle, when I am not at the palace, and I have neglected her. One day she shall have a piano, like a wealthy lady; but she has loved the fiddle since she was a little child. I keep my womenfolk in a first-floor apartment – noisy, of course, but still well-panelled; a sort of nest where they may sew and embroider in peace and quiet. I look at young Mayseder, whose parents are almost gentry – the father some kind of lawyer, with vineyards near Heiligenstadt. Once or twice the boy has talked of revolution, until Ignaz laughs at him. He is a good technician, too, but one who needs to be guided into the music's heart. He eagerly accepts my offer to come along.

So, leaving the palace, we walk upon the sunlit cobbles. Our way is through the Graben, with its smells of kirsch, hashish and coffee. Food is dear but otherwise the occupation changes little. The girls, the Grabennymphen, dart about like damselflies, but just now there are no French soldiers for them to entice or us to avoid. Mayseder, moral and very young, tries not to notice them, as he tries not to notice the maids when we are in the palace. They, of course, make eyes at him. There is a further mingled smell of perfume, and fresh and dried horse-dung, which almost covers the street, and I look forward to climbing the stairs, to where I once more become a family man. Anna will be mending dresses in our cosy room. As I have one floor and no servants I pay less rent than Beethoven does for his windy third-floor garret.

Anna must have heard my step for she comes out onto the landing. I turn to introduce Mayseder, but she has gone suddenly mad:

'Go away,Josef! Please go!'

She clings to my arm, but I fling her aside. A French cavalry officer leaps to his feet as I open the door. His hand is at his belt. Therese sits on the ottoman dressed in creamy silks and satins, with a daisy behind her ear. Mayseder is almost leaning over my shoulder, and Anna is still trying to pull me back. I stand there and wait to be shot. There is a polite veneer to the French occupation, but in private, with the likes of us, they take whatever they want. So I stand and look at my niece as if, or it may really be, for the very last time. Her fledgling breasts don't fit her gown. Her eyes, like a little dog, keep turning towards the Frenchman. Her face is long but not quite oval, longer because her hair is piled up like an aristocrat. I sense that she thinks the soldier handsome, but not quite directly, so to speak; she comes at it through a jumble of thoughts, leading to astonishment, as she does the tune when I am teaching her to play. There is a faint red spot at the side of her mouth.

The Frenchman, black eyes gleaming, moves a chair for Anna beside her, and bows like a ramrod. His uniform is green with red facings and he wears a sabre and a pistol at his belt. He settles himself and picks up a glass. My wine.

'Parlez-vous Francais?' he suddenly raps out.

'Non.' I shake my head.

'Asseyez!' He points me to a chair, and then looks at Mayseder, who slowly nods his head.

I pray that he will be sensible. What if his French gives them a reason to take him for a spy? Beside this officer there is, leaning against the wall, a short, misshapen, leering fellow, fingering a long dagger.

'Asseyez!' Mayseder lowers himself onto the fourth of my chairs. Then the Frenchman speaks, and Mayseder translates as follows:

'This is Captain Eugene Ramballe of the 13th chausseurs. This is his orderly, LeBoeuf. He knew Madame Linke – here - from four years ago, when she was most kind to him…'

Here, I think, he is mistaken, lying or insane. I brought her from Breslau only this spring. Then I look across at Anna and see that I am wrong. She *was* here in 1805. Of course: Johann came with her here before he joined his regiment. And then came Austerlitz…but before the battle the French were also here. This Ramballe was here in Vienna while Johann was still alive. And Anna was here too, in some lodging or other.

'At which time,' Mayseder translates, 'Mademoiselle here was only a *petite jeune fille*.'

Anna's eyes are fixed on me.

'And so, chancing to meet them by the cathedral last week, he has made bold…'

Here Mayseder stops, astonished. He stares wide-eyed at Therese, as if he has just noticed her. Anna's eyes are still fixed on me. What choice, I think, did she have, now or then? Johann had left her behind, alone, and I was in Breslau, busy with my own affairs. I look at her, and see again her great attractions: a buxom, kind-eyed creature, willing and reliable; but it is clear that the Frenchman, whose face, I notice, like mine, already shows the small brown creases of time, has shifted his affections. Unlike me but like many, especially these decadent French who think themselves great lords, he has a taste for virgins.

'And now,' Mayseder continues, after a glare from the Captain, 'he will retire, and come again at a more convenient time.'

The Captain turns his gaze on me. It is ineffably French in the whiteness of the teeth and the studied darkness of the eyes. He bows with the utmost gallantry, and he and the scowling orderly (who, when the Captain's back is turned, makes an obscene suggestion with his dagger), rattle down the stairs.

I should be feeling horror but, instead, I find that same dark, cheerful, and insistent melody running through my mind: Opus 59, first movement. I am aware that Mayseder still cannot take his eyes off Therese. In the end she looks up at us with her pale blue eyes and, intolerably, giggles.

It strikes me, quite suddenly, that I have never really missed Johann, even though his death has left me alone in the world. Even in the monastery we were almost strangers. He was strong. I had this limp. I advanced in learning, and he was left behind. Now, knowing Anna betrayed him – though, I think I believe, she only took the Frenchman in order to feed Therese – I hope that he did not die in pain.

'Is it true?' I ask.

'Yes,' says Anna.

I leave without another word.

Mayseder does an odd thing on the way back. He takes out his fiddle, hands me the case, and there in the Walfischgasse, he plays the adagio, molto e mesto: sublime, but interminable. Suddenly I feel hungry. I gesture him to stop.

'How old is your niece?' he asks. I tell him. She is fourteen. 'I will save her!' he says; and he runs off.

The Rasumovsky palace, open at all hours to Ludwig von Beethoven, draws us together like some especially ill-assorted family. There are, for example, the French librarian and his wife. Madame Bigot plays the piano, but never in public. I imagine she is wary of low musicians. She also has a little girl named Caroline, who seems to occupy her time. Bigot wears round spectacles, and they seem to live like mice; yet Bigot is a great scholar, and they are now planning to return to Paris. Next we have Weiss in his cottage in the grounds, with his boy, Hans – and, of course, with Sophie. Then there are the various secretaries, of whom we take no notice, and the many servants, of whom only one, Natalie, stands out: a plump, blonde, lady's maid who looks German, but is French. She likes me to play to her. In addition Mayseder, and also Schuppanzigh, sometimes stay nights in the attics upstairs. Thus the entire quartet is loosely moored to the Count. I wonder if, in spite of Sophie, he is rather lonely, especially when, as now, Viennese society is completely absent. His wife, the former Countess Thun, is dead, and he is a Russian, without any close ties here except for his strange uncle and his sister-in-law, the famous Princess Lichnowsky, who makes the palace her home when she is in Vienna, with or without her husband. She is expected now – any moment, says Natalie – but I can hardly believe that even she would come in the midst of a battle.

This same day, as the summer twilight deepens, the Rasumovsky quartet comes back into the library. We are not required to wear our livery. The darkening windows catch each candle flame, and the high shelves of books seem to crowd in closer. The windows face north, towards the occupied city; but Russia itself is not at war with France.

Our audience is the Count in his Persian dressing-gown, with Sophie on his right and the uncle on his left. Peter Andreyich has a bulbous, red-veined nose, almost like a small onion, ears that stick from his head like toadstools from a log, a small, purple lower lip, and a bald crown that sits like a helmet over his pale, suspicious eyes. When we begin to play those eyes are watching us all like a hawk. He hears every single note! How we know this I cannot tell, but we all do know. It as if we hear ourselves, joined in one echo, through him.

The Count regards us differently. He would always have this music more firmly within his grasp, and looks on it as a bear in the woods regards a passing cartload of fish.

Sophie sits in her loose bridal garb, her green eyes avidly tranquil; one swollen foot in a satin slipper, and her belly now swollen too. One would suppose she heard nothing. Only when she blinks, as Weiss enters on the viola, might one think otherwise. She, in the Count's finery, has all the self-possession that my poor Therese requires. She knows the Count by now, I think, and, like many a mistress, will not so easily give him the key to her heart.

Yet there is another Sophie besides this puppet: someone brave and bright, who sits with us when we are rehearsing in the ballroom where, further away from the stirrings of the palace, we feel more relaxed; who hums and even sings at her sewing while we play, and makes us laugh and smile when we rest and talk. She is always curious about the other great houses, and can somehow impersonate Archdukes and Princesses whom she has never seen. Yet on one occasion, when the gossip led Schuppanzigh to lower his voice and mention Count Rasumovsky's previous amours she turned into a fury, and noticing a smile upon Weiss's quiet face, she grabbed his bow from him and broke it across her knee. But jealous as she is with the Count, she is jealous with Weiss too: he hardly dares to go to the Schwan.

May 21st

Next day, in the morning, the French begin to march from the city. In the evening we hear some cannon, but Vienna is silent, tense. We know that our army is waiting in the plains to the north of the city, but we are puzzled as to how the French will fight them, since there are no bridges there across the Danube: we hope that they will be swept away, into the river to drown!

May 22nd

Very early on the following day, guns are firing away – firing, firing, in the distance; and, as if guns were quite normal, we and the city begin to stir.

The pounding arouses Natalie, who is in my bed. There are freedoms here not to be found in Breslau. She assures me that Austria will win, but she speaks about it flatly, as if it were no more than a game.

Natalie was right, meanwhile, about Princess Lichnowsky, who arrived last night from the south, given safe passage into the Russian Embassy. Of course she is not up yet. I am thinking again about Anna and Therese: of what, if anything, I should do, and hoping Captain Ramballe has gone, but the palace holds me. I shall forgive Anna, of course, but there is no hurry. In any case there are still French soldiers in the streets.

When I am dressed I peer into the ballroom, and then the empty library. Then I cross the hall, nodding to the porter, and enter, very cautiously, the Count's great Canova room, where Peter Andreyich is busy dusting the statues. There are a dozen great marble figures, antique gods and goddesses, whose eyes look into some unknown world, whose postures plead or threaten, whose naked bodies one can walk all around; and between them goes the old man, like a beetle. He carries with him a black silk cloth with which he dusts the toes, the ankles, calves and knees. He also has a long feather duster which he passes upwards between the thighs, brings down over the marble shoulders, under the armpits and around the gleaming, lifeless breasts. He has with him some wooden steps which he moves with effort and, mounting perilously, flicks away the specks of dust from their marble locks.

Suddenly old Friedrich the porter taps me on the arm:

'Common people, here, Herr Musician, asking to speak with you.'

Behind him is Anna, wrapped in a shawl, and with her is a youth dressed in a plain jacket and breeches. I am about to make some sarcastic comment on Anna's new taste in men, when the youth looks up, and I recognise Therese. Her hair is tightly cropped, and she has the blank, half-sullen expression common to Viennese youth. Behind her back she is grasping her fiddle. Of course I understand at once: Anna hopes that in this disguise she will be taken on in the palace, and hidden from the outside world. If the French captain has gone the people – these Viennese – will be treating her as a whore, and this I had not realised!

A shadow falls between us, and suddenly there is Peter Andreyich, staring hard. I try to make myself see her through his eyes, until I believe that what I see is a pale young boy. His name, I decide, is Fritz. I bow to Peter Andreyich and say:

'He plays Beethoven, your Excellency; plays him very well.'

Peter Andreyich fixes Fritz with his stony eye. Then he shuffles forward, takes the boy's hand and kisses it! His manners are, in their Russian way, exquisite. Now it seems that I can only watch and wait, and hope. Ignoring me, he gestures Fritz to follow, leads us into the hall and shuffles up the great staircase towards the Count's offices. Anna looks pleadingly at me, and then departs.

Bigot and a secretary look up from their pens as the old man shuffles on and opens the inner study door. Here, in a cool room, hung with Italian miniatures, the sun pours into the tops of the orchard beyond, so that one can almost taste the fruit; and here the Count sits behind his desk absorbed in a sheet of paper, while Sophie, in a blue silk morning-gown and slippers, reclines upon a velvet chaise by the opposite wall. The guns have ceased to fire.

Peter Andreyich raps on the desk. Sophie gives him a strangely malevolent look. The Count remains absorbed in his paper until she coughs; then he looks up at us all, smiling at his uncle, glancing vaguely at Fritz and myself, and turning back to Sophie, who lays her hand on her stomach, and points to me with her sharp green eyes. I sense that she is not deceived, even that she is hardly surprised, by Therese's appearance. The hard expression on her face, like those I have seen on soldiers, is strangely at odds with the short, plump body lying there on the couch; but something else has happened since I saw her last night. Her belly is no longer swollen with child. I am afraid that she has miscarried, and when I look at her again and see a little spasm at the corner of her mouth, I am certain of it.

'Have you a request, Herr Linke?' the Count asks affably.

'Your Excellency' I stammer, 'my – nephew Fritz – is looking for employment. He –'

'Plays the violin?'

'Indeed. He has a good deal by heart – Herr Beethoven, Mozart, Haydn.'

'Can you play from sight?'

Fritz nods.

'Well, then, can you play this?'

He turns and pushes the sheet before him across the desk. I see that it is music. Fritz opens the violin and quickly tests the strings; then, leaning forward a little, he plays through the melody.

Peter Andreyich screws up his eyes, but his expression soon becomes morose. This is not Beethoven.

My own gaze strays to the window. Finches are darting below me and through a gap in the leaves I catch sight further off of the fair, unassuming poll of Franz Weiss in his garden. I think I hear the scrape of his hoe, and, despite my anxiety, fear slowly ebbs away. The sound of the violin is delicate, well-balanced, and Therese looks entirely like a young boy at his lesson. We have all become actors, and miracles are possible. The Count leans back with an air of bland abstraction, which makes me certain that this tune is his own composition. Sophie's chin tilts down towards her crooked slippers, as if she has only just noticed her misshapen foot. Before the Count has finished speaking his thanks, she has risen impatiently and taken charge of Fritz. She puts her hand on her belly again as she gestures him to follow, and the Count gives her a sorrowful, bewildered look as the door closes behind them. I bow and take my dismissal, but by the time I reach the staircase they are already gone, and I can only retire to my little room.

***

Natalie brings me a plate of goulash, and I devour it absently. The guns are firing again. How long will the battle last? Austerlitz was over in a single day. Johann has been dead four years. The goulash reminds me of better times, soon after I arrived back in Vienna this spring, with Anna and Therese.

Then I had goulash at the Countess Maria Erdody's, in the Krugerstrasse, where I went to rehearse his new cello sonata with Beethoven. I still glowed inside from the part that he had written for me the year before, in the great Fifth Symphony, and even knowing that he had promised this new piece to Anton Kraft for its first performance could not spoil my pleasure. At least I would be the first to hear it.

Beethoven just then had accepted rooms with the kind little Countess, but his stay with her was often a little turbulent, and that night I arrived in the middle of a row.

'She is your equal!' he was shouting, 'better, if you like! Not your servant – my guest!'

'My dear *mistro*,' twittered the Countess in her Hungarian accent, 'please do not be so angry! Have I not invited her?'

He had an empty soup tureen that in his distraction he had lifted from the table, and was dangling from one thick finger by its handle. The bulge of it was adorned, I think, with Leda and the Swan. I stepped gingerly forward.

'Should she not the wine serve, if she does not object?'

'No!' shouted the Master. 'Ask him!'

He shot out his arm, tureen and all, and I hopped aside as it crashed in pieces.

I looked at Sophie, the cause of the trouble, but it seemed her thoughts were elsewhere.

The little Countess hopped about like a little blackbird, twittering ever faster, laughing, and kicking the pieces aside with her boot. The beige-coloured tureen, she said, had been brought back by her husband, Count Peter, from England, where they have a mania for making them by the dozen. Since he had gone to England again he would probably bring another. It was, almost, the only good evidence of her husband's existence that I had seen, or was ever going to see.

The Countess kissed me. She kissed Beethoven. Last but not least she took the tray from Sophie and kissed her too.

We played the sonata, he and I, in a deep, deep unison. Everything was now at peace. Afterwards Sophie brought over the wine and the glasses on a tray, and the Master did not object. He got up to pour it himself.

There were three of us cripples – I who stump, Sophie who limps, and the Countess who hops like a blackbird. Her apartments are hung with red velvet curtains which keep out most of the draughts. A small fire was burning too, and we felt quite warm.

The talk was of the children – the Countess's boy and girl to whom I had given some lessons. These I had enjoyed more than I expected, and I had found the little Countess with her delicate features and her long, tapering hands very pleasant company. Beethoven asked after Sophie's boy.

'He is well - fourteen years old, that's hard to believe! Yes, he is learning viola and clarinet. He spends,' she added, 'too much time in the palace. The cooks and maids spoil him, when my back is turned.'

'Ah,' sighed the Countess, 'Children, I adore my children. All the same I am only thirty, and I need a little more of…this.'

She picked up a corkscrew and passed it to Beethoven. The bells of St Stephen's cathedral chimed a long way off.

'I'm glad I can have no more,' she said to Sophie, 'but what about you?'

Sophie blushed.

'I am with child, Madame.'

I remember that sentence because, when I told Anna about it, she was shocked and horrified that Sophie would have the Count's child. She was quite sure it *was* the Count's. It was not, she said, for people like us; and I almost felt that, if she had known Sophie better, she would even have said so to her face. I suppose she was jealous that Sophie, another poor woman from Breslau, should live amongst such luxury and power; and jealous too, of course, because I stayed in the palace, or else she was afraid to be on her own too much – a fear that I can now explain. (And now, I think, as I mouth my goulash alone in this little room, it has come to nothing – Sophie has lost that child, and we shall never know what difference it would have made.)

'The Count's sister-in-law,' said Countess Erdody, as if she had not heard, although she had given Sophie's hand a gentle squeeze, 'that is, the Princess Lichnowsky, is often at the Rasumovsky Palace. Very old school - *noblesse oblige*! It is quite amusing to see how the poor Count manages with her.'

Beethoven snorted – he was content – and stated that the lady, though proud, had always been both musical and extremely handsome. Sophie began to bristle, and her green eyes flashed at us as if at some terrible insult, until The Master put out his hand, with its black hairs and powerful fingers, and began to stroke her hair, the nape of her neck, her shoulders, crooning a canon repeatedly, until she began to smile.

'She doesn't care much for *our* music now,' I said, meaning the Princess Lichnowsky, and then wondered why I had spoken. No need for me to add to Sophie's jealous torments, born of the Princess's interest in the Count. Beethoven went on stroking Sophie's hair. Then he began to thoroughly knead her neck, and I could tell he was thinking of some new possible melody, squeezing as he arranged the notes. The Countess smiled at me, and blinked. She poured us each a full glass of wine. A log rolled over and glowed in the fire and, in the silence that followed, creeping from under her brown silk gown, her foot, her good one, as light and purposeful as a blackbird's hop, came out from under her gown and pressed itself on mine.

2: Weiss (21st May, 1809)

Sophie and I get up early to visit Beethoven. Hans is fast asleep. We leave the cottage and cross through the orchard, skirting the formal gardens heavy with the scent of roses, past the ground-floor rooms and through an alley of vines. The orchard slopes gently down to the Donau canal, beyond which stand a handful of shuttered houses, grey and tall as megaliths, their backs to us and their faces towards the rising sun. We take our key which opens a little door in the garden wall, by which we pass into the cool and misty street, and at once St Stephen's spire looms out in the west. It is a good time to feel the splendour of the city, and it is pleasant to walk with Sophie, just like any man and wife. As we approach the bastion, though, we hear shouts in French, and a steady rumble of carts.

These days I would miss Vienna, even if I still hesitate to call it home. I loved it when I came here for that very first rehearsal. But even as we were playing Beethoven here in Vienna my father, who they said refused to move away from the ramparts, died in his church in Breslau. The French bombardment brought it down on him. Sophie, Hans and I went back to a shattered town. After that we came back to Vienna for the winter season, although from Lent to Harvest I played my part, as my father's son, in the Lutheran brotherhood of Breslau. They paid me what they could afford. Even before that first return the Count would also send for Sophie, when he took rooms in the new Oder Inn, on his way to or from Teplitz, Karlsbad, Moscow or St Petersburg, and she could not refuse: he needs her. He loves her and she loves him; but she still loves me. So she leads the double life more often led by those of high rank - demanding, moreover, his loyalty and mine. The Count of course leads a double life too - in public the quiet widower. The night before last she spent with him, and returned in the morning exhausted. Last night she slept by me. In spite of the shadows they cast – his greatness, her strange moods - it's a relief to have settled here in Vienna for ever, or for how long God wills. It is good to play with Schuppanzigh, Linke and Mayseder, and sometimes to fill a place in the orchestra too. I must make the best of what I did not choose.

Beethoven has long been up, and greets us without surprise. He makes no comment on the noise below although, as always, his window is wide open. The clamour and bustle – and one or two shrieks – come from every direction at once, but his mind is elsewhere, and his poor hearing probably muffles the noise.

Sophie lays down the clothes he left with us to be laundered, when he was on his way to play duets with Madame Bigot. Now he looks at Sophie with an erection poking up his nightshirt.

'*Pom-pom, pom-pom, pom pom pom*!'

He shouts and laughs and lifts one foot.

Sophie looks into his eyes and he squeezes up his brows.

'Look at your belly, like a fat sparrow! Come close, I like to hear you chirp. He kisses her and sniffs her hair. Then he turns to me.

'Be good to her, Franz Weiss, for all her faults. Remember that we are all miserable sinners.

Now, play this for me!'

Breathless and astonished I open up my instrument.

'You won't need the bow!'

I look up, uncomprehending.

'Pizzicato, friend! Look here!'

He holds up the sheet of music. I begin to pluck the strings. *Plink-plink, plink-plink, plink plink plink* . I read ahead through the bars.

'Like a harp,' I say.

'What are you doing?' he howls at Sophie.

She is picking up his soiled clothes from the floor. Her face is flushed with effort. He leaps across the room and hurls them onto his desk. I notice the stale smells – clothes, food, and a whiff of urine – whirled up in a last morning breeze before the summer heat sets in. There is a scurry of heavy boots below. French soldiers, on the move. Beethoven puts his hand under Sophie's arm and sits her down carefully on his rickety chair.

'Madame Sophie, what was I thinking? And you, Weiss, too, must think of the child. Here, take her home. I must find a servant, as soon as the damned French leave. Now go. Go-go-go!'

'*Plink-plink-plink*,' we hear him shouting. '*Plink-plink*, *plink-plink*, **plink plink plink**!'

The air in the street is close and fetid. Sophie holds the dirty bundle over her swollen belly.

***

Fifteen years ago: the market-place at home. I had been sent to buy something. In France the people had cut off the King's head. It did not seem possible. She was a Polish orphan, limping, with those green eyes, like a maimed but fearless kitten. She was begging in broken German, asking sharply 'Will you give me some food?' She kept it up for an hour, while the women scoffed and the men crept up like vultures. In the end I did pluck up the courage to speak to her.

'My father is the pastor, here in Breslau,' I said. 'We are Lutherans, but he will give you shelter.' So then we married, and Sophie kept house for my father and I. Soon she gave birth to Hans. Nine or ten years passed like a dream. My father taught Hans the clarinet, and I gave lessons to keep us.

***

There is no bustle now in the city, no sound from the citizens. And the reason dawns on me: the French are leaving Vienna! Sophie walks on slowly. A clock somewhere strikes nine.

As we turn a corner we are suddenly faced with a troop of French Cavalry. I duck, pulling Sophie with me, into a doorway. She looks out from inside my arms, and I can feel her eyes darting among the uniformed men, who sit on their horses as motionless as toys. The sun beats down on them. Sophie's curls of red-brown hair tumble over her damp white neck. Holding her close arouses me. It is like a dream, except for the horses' breathing and the noises in the distance – the shouting and the beating of drums, as this troop waits with hardly a stir.

A two-wheeled calèche appears, hood down, driven by an officer. Behind him sits a surly, sly, stupid, cheerful rogue, and by his side is a fair-haired girl in white, a waif whose fingers, which are exceedingly long, dangle over the side of the carriage. Then I hear a violin. It is the adagio from the first Rasumovsky quartet, the one we played the other night. I look up and see Josef Mayseder across the street; fair-haired and gawky, but dressed in black as if for a public concert. The fair-haired girl looks up and smiles. I see she cannot help herself. The officer brings his horses to a stop. The girl stands up and starts to mime a violin. I can almost see it as she mimes the bow, as she mimes precisely the fingering of this passage, almost as Schuppanzigh might play it. There is grace in her action, in spite of her thin white arms. 'Beautiful,' I say aloud. Sophie turns and thrusts the dirty clothes at me. Now Mayseder stands close by them, and the little rogue begins to shout. The officer turns to look and jumps down with his whip in his hand. The little rogue pretends to draw his sword across his throat. Then, I don't know how, Sophie is between Mayseder and the Frenchman. Gently and yet forcefully she puts her hands upon his strings and forces his bow to stop. The officer smiles now under his black moustaches; beckoning to Sophie, he brings the girl down from the carriage. He says a few words in her ear while Sophie takes her by the hand, and speaks in her other ear. I stand holding the bundle of clothes.

Now the tall, dark officer shouts an order. The men stir; their harness jingles; the whole troop moves off at a trot. But the girl escapes from Sophie, races off on her skinny legs, penetrates the cloud of dust, and jumps back inside the calèche. The officer lifts his arms aloft, whether in triumph or despair I cannot tell, and then there is nothing left but the hot sun and the settling dust.

Mayseder has disappeared. We walk on slowly towards the palace. Sophie pauses once or twice and puts her hand on her swollen belly. As we are walking in silence I wonder about young Mayseder, and then about the girl in white who recognised that melody. She has changed since I last saw her, but it can only be Therese, Anna Linke's daughter, and the reason she knows the music is that Linke has taught her this quartet. I stop still in front of the palace, and tell Sophie my thought.

'Of course she is,' she says.

'Then should we not tell Linke?' Sophie shakes her head. The Frenchman, she says, the officer, understands that the girl must be returned. It is unlucky that she became entangled with him, but she cannot stray far. She must ask the Count to help.'But will he really help?'

'Oh yes,' she says. 'Even, if need be, in his own person. He knows that officer. The girl is a silly little fool, that's all.'

'But if they are going to war?' I ask. Sophie shakes her head and does not reply.

We are back in the palace garden, under the apple trees again, and suddenly she touches me and yields me up a kiss. 'Be quick,' she says, 'I have work to do.' She pulls me in by the back door, where I drop the clothes, and bends serenely forward for me upon the black oak table in our little room; my wife.

***

At midday I meet Schuppanzigh at the Countess Erdody's apartment, which is occupied by French officers of the general staff, tall and stately men of high rank. One of them, the Baron de Tremont, comes over to speak to Ignaz, who introduces me. I gather he has met Beethoven. Ignaz translates that he is charmed to meet the husband of Madame Weiss. He has been shown the Canovas and taken tea with the Count and Madame in the library. The Baron hopes that we shall not be interrupted by news of the battle. He tells us, politely, that The Emperor is in the field. We hasten to play a programme of excerpts; of all Vienna has to offer. The tenor Rockel sings Florestan's great aria from 'Leonore': the husband confined in chains and dreaming of his wife. Our audience are clearly moved to pity, though afterwards they ask the meaning of one or two German words.

Walking back towards the palace I hear behind doors and

windows a constant smothered bustle and clattering of pails, as the richer sort of people recover their misused houses from the French. Of course, they may return. Some of the shops are open, but everyone I see looks warily about. Far away to the north there are occasional sounds of cannon.

Suddenly I begin to walk away towards the Danube, in the very direction the French army has taken. I do not expect to find the girl. I will, I think, just go a little way, and then turn back. But, before I realise, I am walking through the orchards that lead down to the river. There are places here where the grass has been trampled flat, but there are no soldiers. Unlike those in the Count's gardens, newly transplanted and straight, the apple trees here are crooked and neglected, but there is blossom on the long spurs, low to the ground and high in the air. I can now see the river. Then suddenly, between the branches, I make out her white dress, and then I hear her singing - 'La---la--la, la': infinitely sad. I move closer, and now she sees me. But now I hear the noise of a carriage on the road. I turn and see the Count's new landau, driven by a huge, pock-marked fellow, and in it the Count and Sophie, shading their eyes and looking out. It moves towards the river, turns and passes back again. Both I and the girl have hidden ourselves in the trees.

'It's not safe!' says Linke's niece, with an odd wag of her head as I come up to her. She is on her hands and knees. Her eyes are washed with tears. When she stands I see the grass-stains on her satin dress.

'Not safe?' I say. 'It's quiet enough!' Far off there are faint explosions, and once or twice what might be a scream, but they seem to come from another world. Away to my left the bank is churned up. There are broken planks, a shako or two, and a dead horse buzzing with flies Little waves on the river sparkle in the sun. The sounds in the distance seem to come from beyond a bend, where willow trees stand tall on an island. Somewhere over there, I guess, the French Army has gone across.

She is tall – as tall as me, or Linke, or Mayseder; not so tall as the Count, or the Frenchman she was with. Her hands make little puppet-gestures.

'Come,' I say, 'I'll take you back home.' I hold out my hand, as one does to a child, but I have to stop. She is stiff and staring and pale. I stand there for a while, not moving, and then, slowly, not to alarm her, sit myself down on the grass. I think she partly recognises me, but it is as though that dress, which should belong to a Duchess's child, confuses all her thoughts. I look at the sky, the water and the apple-blossom. I will bide my time.

***

It was only two years ago in Breslau, at about this time of year, that Linke came back from Vienna. He had been to the farm and brought Anna and her daughter to our house. The old people, he said, were out of temper. He told us of the little apartment he had found for them, one day. Then he travelled on to Prince Lichnowsky at Gratz, where he had been asked to rehearse the rag-bag orchestra. Schuppanzigh had suggested him. The Prince and Princess had had a fearful quarrel with Beethoven the year before.

Sophie, Anna and I sat outside, drinking wine at the table with our neighbour Stepan and his brother. Our house, which they had helped us repair, was next to the ruined church where they found my father. He is buried under the chancel. It is a very quiet spot now, with the broken town wall half-open to the Oder and the plain beyond. Little ripples of cool air came by us as the sun went down. Sophie was making Stepan laugh. My foot was touching Anna's. Her long brown hair lay by my arm. I think I said something – some nonsense – and we smiled. And then I was absolutely and entirely overwhelmed by my need of her. Our hands touched, then clasped. I made an excuse to stand up – I could feel her eyes, her breath, as I turned around – and then I was sitting beside her on the bench while Sophie still joked with Stepan. It was as if one flame were licking at us both. Unable, quite, to kiss, we were dissolving into each other. Her hair was against my face. Our hands touched again, and our knees and hips melted together like gold.

When we had all gone indoors I waited for Sophie to fall asleep and then, even more on fire, I crept downstairs to Anna. The little girl, Therese, was lying beside her asleep but I did not care. Then Sophie came down and drove us apart, and Anna was gone next morning.

***

Therese sits a little way off. I can tell that she is breathing more quietly. As if to myself, I slowly begin to talk about the new quartet I saw this morning. It will be serene, I say to myself, and perfect as the others. I hum the few bars of pizzicato, making a noise like a hen, and then I sing the same tune Therese was singing when I arrived, from the adagio of the first Rasumovsky: 'La---la---la, la' : infinitely sad.

Then I talk about quartet playing - the practice, and the hours when one reflects on why that note sounds wrong. I tell her of the boredom as well as the joy, the liveries and the great houses where we eat with the cooks. I talk of the choir in Breslau, where we played nothing but Bach. I am looking at the ripples on the stream, the far-off sun behind St Stephen's and the blossom on the trees. Flies buzz loudly around the dead horse.

I speak again of the quartets, of my favourite scherzo in the first, and I start to mime my part, letting my fingers clutch the air. She smiles and watches, and after a minute she too lifts a pretend fiddle. She knows this movement too! Her smile is like the summer sky. Again, she moves her arms and legs in an unconscious puppet-dance. Then she droops forward and her face falls.

'He was a Count,' she says, 'before their revolution.' It is her way of saying he has gone. Even if he returns he will not be looking for her. I suppose he told her something here, under the apple-trees. But if she goes home now and people see her in that gown there is no telling what they might do; they will want their revenge out of the French, and her. We must wait for dusk. And so we wait while muffled sounds continue to drift across the river.

As we return at last the darkness comes on quickly. There are torches about in the streets. Through open windows there are the sounds of clinking glasses, cutlery. I persuade her to put her arm around me, with her head down; and we mimic, as best we can, some other couples in the street, swaying across the dark cobbles: but one woman passing by, a ragged, stooped old witch, looks up vindictively and spits in Therese's face.

Anna is looking out for us, and, in what seems less than a moment, Therese has been given some brandy and put to bed. Anna gives me the rocking chair and sits down on the ottoman, and we look shyly at one another by the dim light of a lamp. I am in the one place Sophie has forbidden me: should Linke ever ask me to come here, she said, I must refuse. I wonder what my life would be now if I had run away with Anna that night, taking her and Therese, leaving Sophie and Hans, seeking a new life somewhere – where? Weimar? Prague? So many places I will never see. Only those French soldiers, I suppose, have seen so many places. Anna's hair is tied up, but I can tell that it is still of silky brown.

'And how – how is Sophie?' she asks. She is well, I tell her; expecting. Anna nods. I can see she already knows. Her eyes are not, as I thought, a light brown, but more of a luminous grey. She tells me she has heard there are positions in the palace. The whole of the neighbourhood saw her daughter with the French Captain; whether he returns or not, she will not be safe. It is my turn to nod. If I can help in any way Anna has only to let me know. Should I speak to Linke, or Sophie? Anna shakes her head: not yet.

As I depart she places a hand on my arm. The fingers are warm and quick: a needlewoman's hands. She is still so very desirable, but I resist.

'After this war,' she says, 'we'll meet again, as friends.' I nod. I would like to do that, but I have Hans and Sophie to think of. And Sophie's approval would somehow have to be gained. So I only nod, and give back only half of her gentle smile. As I walk away in the darkness I turn my thoughts to my own troubles. Hans is about to leave us. I don't want to lose my son and he doesn't want to go, but Sophie has made the decision and she has good reasons. Prince Lichnowsky is always in need of musicians at his estate, where every household servant plays one instrument or another. Hans will receive a little money as well as clothes and food; more importantly he will learn his trade, much as I did in the church. At fourteen he is far too young and inexperienced to play in Vienna's orchestras. Besides, as Sophie points out, there are too many temptations in the palace, even for a boy his age. He is growing chubby from his visits to the kitchens. At Prince Lichnowsky's the fare is plain. The servants there will be more wholesome company than the Count's cooks and maids. Therefore, though I love to see his freckled, open face, tousle his red hair and feel his affectionate hugs, the Count has made the arrangement, and I have agreed. I shall miss trying to teach him (although I wish he would show more application), but in Gratz he will have a reason to practice both viola and clarinet. Princess Lichnowsky, when she arrives, may stay here a week or a month; but when she returns to Gratz, Hans is to ride on the coach. I was teaching him in the cottage last week, when he suddenly said:

'It's because of her baby. Hers and the Count's. Disgusting!' He took the viola – a gift of the Count's - and swung it over his head by the scroll.

'Hans!' I cried.

'Hans, Hans!' he mocked me – but put the viola down. 'We should do like the French. Kill all the *junkers*, especially the foreign ones.' His face was both red and sullen. Then a tear squeezed from his eye.

'You don't believe that, Hans.'

I reached out and ruffled his hair. I waited. He had not noticed the tear.

'Are you all right now?' I asked.

'Oh,' he shrugged and put out his hand so that it nearly touched mine, 'I am better than you.' Now I vow, as I walk through the dark, restless streets, that in future I will not let my son see the feelings of impotence which sometimes make me tremble. Everything is as it is, and I must try to be content.

As if, somehow, the time were still not right yet to return, I turn aside to the bastion, and climb the steps. There is a rumble far off again. Having seen where their army crossed I wish to see or hear what I can of the battle that is going on out there in the dark. I go cautiously up until I reach the parapet. The old stone wall is half a ruin, encroached on by the newer houses. In the moonlight I can see the hills in the distance, and a white church tower, and before them a moving darkness where fires flicker and smoke rolls like quiet waves. There is a crack, and something, a bullet, whizzes past my head. French voices call from below. I scramble down and hurry off into the streets, wondering at my foolishness.

A coach is drawn up outside the palace. I recognise the arms on its side. Count Rasumovsky jumps from his horse – he must have ridden to meet her -and opens it for Princess Lichnowsky. I recognise her swathe of black hair, and the way she twitches her shoulders. She takes the Count's offered arm and hurries with him up the wide stairs.

I slip around to the side-street and into the orchard, and stand for a minute, observing the drifts of moonlight that catch the apple-trees, the parterres, the houses beyond the Donau, and our little cottage. Only now do I realise that I will have to account for myself. I will say that I have been with Schuppanzigh all day, and hope for the best. Believing, rightly or wrongly, that Princess Lichnowsky has designs on the Count, Sophie will not be in a happy mood. Also, she did not find Therese, and I dare not tell her she is safe. And lastly, though it is her idea, preparing for Hans's departure will trouble her. I take a deep breath and go inside.

Hans is sitting downstairs. His face is white with fear. I look at him for a moment in silence, and then Sophie's terrible wailing breaks out again upstairs. I do my best to comfort her. I think I do, but comfort is impossible. All the life has gone from her face. At last, as the sky lightens, and the cannon still sound far off, I go out into the garden and bury the still-born girl-child. It is Sophie's wish, to have her buried there. I mound up the earth, not looking, and cut a few turves to place on top.

3: Mayseder (22nd-23rd May 1809)

I would have them all shot: or a guillotine for the highborn women, and blindfolds too. An easy death, they say. My father used to say, imagine – imagine the guillotine standing outside St Stephen's. The people kneeling down, the Hapsburgs on the scaffold. 'Why are we kneeling?' I said. But my father, like Louis von Beethoven, whom I will *not* call 'The Master', as some do, has also changed his mind. Gunpowder frightens them both, and neither of them has the stomach to fight for freedom and equality; of course I don't want bloodshed either, but the Junkers will never stop treating us as slaves of their own free will. Right now, between the tyranny of Bonaparte and that of our own masters, we are further from freedom than ever. My father has paid the French a levy to be left in peace, and has added ten cases of last year's wine to be safe. Everyone who can afford it does the same, though some prefer to make an officer their guest. Yesterday morning I guessed correctly which way those chausseurs would pass, after our neighbours told us their officer was leaving for battle. I was not afraid to die in the street – to die for music and Therese's innocence, or to rescue her and take her home with me – yet I found myself going home alone, to find my mother and sisters talking about the dresses they ordered before the French arrived.

And in spite of everything I must be at the palace this afternoon! I set off again, fiddle-case in hand, with the Count's warrant in my pocket in case I should be stopped. I pass through the Graben again, hoping to avoid a hand on my arm, a whisper in my ear. Those hot, silky sirens bleed Viennese men of their will – among them, I suspect, both Beethoven and my father. Therese is the opposite: her purity will give me strength. But here there are the foul smells and that distant rumble like thunder, and an unbearable tension in the heavy air, even though the shops and inns are open. I hope that

French Captain, Ramballe, never returns from battle. I hate the French being here, and yet they are the troops not only of Bonaparte, but of the common people. I think I hate my own people more. Austrians care only for food and drink, like old Schuppanzigh. Meanwhile the Junkers do as they have always done, treating us like dirt. Of course they abandoned Vienna long before the French arrived. There is more truth in *Figaro* than *Leonore-Fidelio*, and not much in either. Here is Weiss, for example, prostituting his wife (what was she doing yesterday, with the Frenchman?), except he has no choice; and how can any amount of music make up for that?

Jean-Jacques Rousseau says: "When there is a riot or a street brawl the populace gather while the prudent man walks away; it is the rabble, the marketplace women, who separate the combatants and prevent decent people killing each other." I know what he means: fraternity. The trouble is that in the palace, in the city under the French, even among us musicians, it is every man for himself. Bonaparte comes here with his army, and the Count, his Russian ally, sits in his palace like some old spider, watching on. I enter the palace and wait in his Canova room, disturbed by the silent presence of his naked statues, until Sophie finds me out. I make her a mock aristocratic bow. She puts her hands on her stomach. I do not understand Sophie. She stands with her crippled foot among the naked figures, her face like blood-red wine. The far-off cannon can still be heard, but she makes no comment. Yesterday she stepped in like one of those market-women, seeming to throw a spell even over the French, but today she looks coldly on me, on everything. She beckons, and I follow her up the stairs. She moves with an effort, with one hand on the marble banister, looking down at the blood-red carpet beneath her feet. On the landing she pauses a moment and puts her hand to her stomach again. I notice how attractive she is, in her apparent clumsiness: I do not feel the corruption that I know exists. I see that her housekeeper's dress is made of a fine dark silk; but I feel that underneath it she is very unhappy. We pass the Count's offices, and climb the narrow, wooden stairs that lead to the attics, and we come to the room in which

I sometimes stay after the Count's late concerts, when with Schuppanzigh and Linke, I go down to the kitchen and we sit with Natalie, and eat and drink and talk all night and I sit in the corner, out of the way. Mostly Schuppanzigh leaves us, drunk, in the early morning, but now and then he follows me, breathing hard, up here. Sophie takes a key from her pocket and unlocks my door. I had never noticed that it had a lock. Then she turns and stares at me hard.

'You are to have a friend,' she says, 'a young lad I want you to help.'

'And what if I refuse?' I answer. Am I to be dictated to because she is the Count's whore?

'Be careful,' she says, 'remember who pays you. Also I know that you wrote to certain *political* students at Dresden...'

'No!' I exclaim. 'You don't know. How?'

'I think Prince Metternich passed your letter on to the Count. He thinks that the Count should be careful whom he employs.'

I stare again and the lower half of her face breaks into a grin.

'Relax,' she says. 'The Count doesn't care. Now – 'She throws open the door.

'Get up!' she calls to the boy, who is lying on the furthest bed – the one on which I sleep, but I see that the other has also been made up.

'Fritz – this is Josef. He will be like a brother to you; and he will let me know,' she adds, with a sideways look, 'if anyone causes you trouble, or if you cause any. I will leave you to get acquainted, but in an hour I will send for you both.'

Sophie is gone, and I look more closely at this youth, who is now standing against the wall as if he would shrink into it. He jigs, nervously, on one foot before returning my stare. I look at the shape of the mouth and nose, and then into the pale blue eyes, and feel my own mouth opening: I am about to exclaim 'Therese!', to rush to her and kiss her hand, to formulate a plan of escape – but something about her stops me. She looks so young she could really be a boy, and I remember Linke telling me her age – fourteen. It was her adorable innocence and danger that made me worship her, and worship her I do; but she is safe here and I, as her lover, must wait. I will wait gladly! I could almost bless Sophie. Then I think of how the Frenchman smiled at her, and I become suspicious. Does Sophie know that fellow? Could she even be keeping Therese here against his return? That seems possible – the Count, of course, has dealings with the French – but then Linke, who is a fool but not a beast, would also know that his niece is in the palace. He would want to protect her. I must find out what Linke thinks, and be on my guard in any case. Perhaps I will get a dagger.

I look at Therese again. She is already dressed in the Count's livery and, with her eyes cast down, she really is the picture of a serving-boy. I must convince myself for now that serving-boy is what she is. I must act as if she were. In that way I shall guard her as Sophie has commanded, and better. I look around the bare room with two beds in opposite corners. On the wall facing the window hang two faded tapestries. One shows Actaeon watching Diana; the other he turned to a stag. Pretending to yawn, I stretch myself out on my bed, and watch through half-closed lids as not Therese but Fritz, the new serving-boy, cautiously does the same. We lie like this until Natalie knocks and tells us both to bring our fiddles downstairs. Although they sit in their usual seats the Count, Sophie and Peter Andreyich look washed-out in the library. Dust-motes float by the window, towards the endless rows of books. While Peter Andreyich stares relentlessly at Fritz, the Count squeezes Sophie's hand.

Weiss and Linke both look troubled. The scores lie out on our stands. We are to play from sight. There is no Schuppanzigh, and now I learn that I am to play first violin, and that Fritz will play second. Already, in this small assembly, Therese has ceased to exist, and there is only Fritz. I pray that he is capable.

There is a smell of warm leather, of musty books and coffee, as we endure a string quartet composed by the Count himself; as tiles on the rooves outside shimmer as blankly as one bar succeeding the next, and Peter Andreyich looks on, expressionless but far from rapt. The rest of us are taut and tense – and still, far off, there is a distant echo of guns.

Rasumovsky's third and fourth movements are no more than sketches – besides which I think they owe not a little to Haydn. The allegro is a Mozart tune, and not one of his best. The andante is a triumph of diplomacy in notes. Yet, I think, it *could* succeed, if it were less cobwebby. *I* could do something with it. As we play the final chord I look again at Sophie's face. There are blotches now on her cheeks. She looks across, directly, at Weiss. Her eyes flash green as they rove beyond us, up to the ceiling and rows of books. She seems to be angry once more. The Count looks sideways at her, as if to know what she thinks of his composition; but in that pause, as we lower our bows, the door is flung open, and in rushes Beethoven! He is flourishing sheets of paper, his hair is sticking out, and there are remains of   dinner on his coat.

'Well, Beethoven!' smiles the Count. 'Drinks!' he says to Sophie. She gets up and hobbles, scowling, away.

'You have something there?' he enquires of the composer, who is following Sophie's retreat with a distracted gaze. Of course he has to go closer and repeat the question.

'Ah, your highness! If I might beg you – something for the Archduke, in fact.   Your man said the players were here. A new quartet! I have all the parts, I wrote them out myself. If you would be so kind…' - he is handing the music round – 'You Count, will you play second? But - no Schuppanzigh today?'

'Sadly not,' lies the Count, whom I credit with the instinct to keep Schuppanzigh away from what he has perpetrated, 'we were merely diverting ourselves. I need not play, however: we shall put these two young gentlemen to the test. They have been practising just now.'

Beethoven looks askance at Fritz and I.

'*Him* I know. Can the other play?'

'In my judgement, yes.'

In Dresden there are people, students, who believe in freedom. Here a battle is being fought in the distance, but we are caught in the palace; cut off and trapped like flies in a web. Sophie returns with her silver tray, ice-bucket with champagne and three glasses, and sets them down before the Count. I feel as if we must explode – and then we begin to play. For half an hour the world is hushed – allegro (pizzicato), adagio, presto and allegretto – all made in one piece of sweet sublimity. Weiss, for some reason, has been grinning like a ferret since we began.

It is hard to believe that the man watching with stubborn, deaf concentration, can have produced this miracle. It is like Opus 59 in power and fluidity and soaring imagination – even, in my mind, excelling them – so calm, clear, joyful, and serious, in spite of the *plink-plink-plink*.

The Count jumps up to shake Beethoven's hand.

'A masterpiece!' He can say no less. 'A drink now, and then duty calls…'

Another smooth lie, I think.

'I thank your excellencies!' Beethoven bows profusely to the four of us.

The Count responds by pouring champagne for him and Peter Andreyich. Beethoven, elated, holds up his glass:

'To us – no, to England, the capital of Music!' He grins, and downs it all in one go.

'To Peace,' the Count says amiably. '*You*, my friend, are the capital of Music!' He pauses, and then asks in French:

'But did they play it well?' I suppose he would like to blame the defects of *his* composition on our inexperience, or to convince himself that playing through from sight could not do it justice. But Beethoven does not answer. He has not heard.

The Count smiles and nods at Sophie. She puts her head to one side then limps across and says loudly in Beethoven's ear:

'The Count asks if they played it *well*?'

'What? Who?'

The *Count!*' she suddenly screams, so that Beethoven's eyebrows lift and his body rocks like a boulder, 'asks if they played it *well.*'

I think that the glass will break inside his fist. His thick brows twitch with pain. But he turns away from Sophie and looks at the Count with flashing eyes.

'Ja,' he says, in his thickest German, 'they played it well enough. And yet – ' he looks at Fritz and I – 'these *trouser-*

33

buttons have not suffered enough. Not battle-scarred like us, eh Linke? Not full of tears like Weiss! I should say that all in all they played it like – *ambassadors.*'

'Ha!' says the Count, 'what did I tell you? But I shall also ask my court! You – he turns to Sophie – 'were the violins not good?'

But Sophie looks away and will not answer. She is holding her stomach.

'And you, Uncle?' Rasumovsky goes up excitedly to the old man, and points at us.

Peter Andreyich, ghoulish, forgotten, totters forward. He comes up close to Fritz. He smiles. Then he slowly shakes his head.

'Ah well,' smiles the Count, repossessing himself, 'you must come back tomorrow. Schuppanzigh will be here. Then the Rasumovsky will play!'

'But is Marie not here?' Beethoven says suddenly, as if he were a child. He and Sophie are collecting up his scores. 'Marie?' the Count frowns. 'I do not think…'

'Madame Bigot,' says Sophie. 'Yes, she is here still. They are packing, of course…'

'I must say farewell, then,' says the Master, sadly. 'I did not really think that they would go back to Paris. Farewell Marie, and Bigot! Farewell Caroline, you pretty little girl!'

'Weiss,' the Count says stiffly, 'take your wife away. She weeps.' It is true: Sophie is weeping, and her face is a desolate wreck. Fritz and I leave the library last, after Linke has patted him on the shoulder. We pass back along the corridor, and make our way up the great staircase; but on the landing we are confronted by Princess Lichnowsky. She is almost as tall as the Count himself, with pronounced shoulders and hips, a tall white forehead, narrow face and, this afternoon, an undressed mane of black hair which makes her look like a restive horse. She lifts her upper lip in the appearance of a smile:

'Ah, Herr Mayseder, a word!' She casts a glance at Fritz, who I am holding by the arm.

'You, boy. You may go!' She follows him with her eyes for a moment, and I am afraid she will notice something. When he is not jigging his steps are very smooth, and the red livery makes it more conspicuous; but no-one would notice that unless they already knew.

'Ah,' the Princess says again, 'Herr Mayseder - a word!' It is like the repeated snort of a horse, looking me over.

'I am at your Highness' service.'

'Ah,' she says, pointing along the landing, 'that dreadful von Beethoven is here, ungrateful man, shouting at those French peasants – ' I stare at her, astonished.

'I mean those Bigots, whose child makes noise underneath my floor! But no matter; we shall have peace, and then the Count has promised a ball!'

There, on the landing, she executes a step, and I am half afraid that she will miss her footing, tumble down and break her neck. I feel as if I want to stretch out a hand, and pacify her. She chuckles as she informs me that, for this ball, I am to write a new dance in her honour. What kind of dance, it seems, is up to me. And when, I ask humbly, does she think that it will be required? She smiles at me again, with her mixture of warmth, pride and insanity. I wonder that the Count, in his vanity, would try out his quartet while she is here, for she would certainly hear its faults. I know – it was never a secret - that the Lichnowskys have quarrelled with Beethoven, or he with them; but before that they were his greatest noble friends. It was my father who sold the horse which the Prince inadvisedly gave to Beethoven as a present.

'When there is peace,' replies the Princess. Holding her skirt, she comes so close that I can smell the lavender in her bosom. 'When we make friends again with the Tsar and the devil Bonaparte is beaten. And tonight,' she adds sharply, as if she has just remembered, 'you shall come with me. Bring your instrument. You shall play what you please.'

'Where to, your Highness?'

'Never mind. Be ready at six.'

Fritz is lying face down, dejected, on my bed. With an effort of will I see him still as a young boy, overwhelmed, as any would be, by the scenes we have witnessed downstairs. It is true that he played a little apart from the rest of us – he has not learned to catch the ball. I must try to help him with that, if he plays again; it will be my way of serving the young girl that I adore in my thoughts; the young girl who has disappeared, who will one day return my love. The stranger things become in this palace, the more this boy will need my help. He lies there, twitching a little, and I know that he knows his playing was not quite right. I run across the room, punch him on the shoulder and cry:

'They are just fools you know! I will teach you how to please them. Come on, be a man!'

He rolls over and grins. I am too close to those blue eyes and that small, soft mouth. In order to suppress my feelings I make a play of boxing his ears, which causes him to squeal and plunge off the bed. Leaning over I suddenly find that he has come right under it and sits on the floor beside my legs. I sit up and look down at him. It is not so difficult now to convince myself that he is a boy. I put my hand out cautiously and stroke his tousled head. The hair is soft and a little springy, just like my own, but the touch makes me feel dizzy. To steady myself I pinch his neck. I grip his shoulder. My hand slips onto his chest and I feel him stiffen. Now I don't know how to act: I should leave him, perhaps, until my feelings are properly under control; but I don't want him to feel unhappy and alone. I close my eyes, relax my arms, and lean back against the bolster. It will come to me in a minute.

He is leaning against my right leg. As I am lying there I think I feel him turn towards me and then I feel his slender fingers on my waist. He is kneeling towards me. I open my eyes for a moment, then close them, and put my hand back on his head. In a swift movement he takes me into his mouth and does things with his tongue until, with one long gasp, I explode.

When I open my eyes again he is on the other bed. His tunic is buttoned up, and some sheets of music are sticking out from under the pillow. I can see from here that it is the Count's quartet. He lies there expressionless. I want to ask if he is all right. I cannot ask him anything. The image of a young girl pleasuring the French Captain with his black moustaches and his lascivious smile floats relentlessly through my mind; I see her long hair falling across his thigh. With an effort I look at Fritz. I must teach him that such things are not what *I* want, but I can't begin it now. I have to take off my dark clothes and put on my own red livery. The Princess will expect it. I feel better, somehow, for being dressed like a servant too. I wash my face and hands from the jug and basin. The water is not too cold. As I go to the door I turn around to him.

'How did you get that score?' I ask.

'I made too many copies,' he says. 'I had to copy them this morning, and I made four, as well as the Count's.'

'You must be tired then, Fritz?'

He nods, his eyes sorrowful.

'Hungry?' He shakes his head.

***

Once again I am waiting in the Canova room. The statues seem to be watching my back. Before too long I hear Princess Lichnowsky humming, the rap of her heels and swish of her skirts, and then I follow her down the palace steps and into her huge barouche. Peter Andreyich appears, assisted by the new coachman, a huge, pock-marked ruffian, who makes me think of the portrait of Danton. The fellow throws me a savage look, as if he divines my thought, before climbing up and driving us through the quiet streets. There is still the distant rumble of artillery and a far-off whisper that might be musket-fire. When we pass a group of French soldiers the Princess looks at them and sniffs.

A footman is waiting for us at the Burg, helping down Peter Andreyich, who is dressed in his usual black frock-coat. The Princess wears a dark red dress and a black cloak. She turns to me and says sharply: 'Please ensure that you observe the manners of your place. Prince Metternich is scrupulous.'

I have been too wrapped up in my thoughts even to care where we are going, but now her words strike fear into my heart. In the letter I wrote to the students at Dresden, which of course was intercepted, I said I admired their struggle for freedom; I should not have used the word struggle, which could be taken to mean revolution. And now I am here at the Burg, where there are guards and dungeons! I pray that I have been forgotten. I am nothing but the Princess's musician, and Prince Metternich, our ambassador to France, surely has no time to think of anything but this war. As we enter we are bowed to by several men in dark coats. Among them I am relieved to recognise Zmeskall, of the Hungarian Chancellery, an urbane *bon viveur* who is Beethoven's friend, and also Carl Beethoven, the wealthy younger brother, who works in the Treasury. Beside them is a tall, gaunt fellow who looks far more dangerous. But I am far too conspicuous in the Count's red livery, which clashes most horribly with Prince Metternich's yellow coat. His hair is fair and quite long – altogether he looks like some young knight of German legend. 'Ah,' he says, as I bow low, 'the promising composer.' I pray he is not dissimulating – and it is true that I have a name for a few marches and waltzes – but he gives such a friendly bow, playing with his seal of office, that I almost feel at home, even as I am dismissed to join the other hangers-on.

The room is cool and dim and noiseless. The walls are stone, the doors iron-studded. Where Prince Metternich sits with Peter Andreyich and the Princess, there are velvet-covered chairs and carpets on the stone floor. For everyone else there are plain chairs along the wall by the great, empty hearth. Once or twice a messenger brings Metternich a note. Wine is served, but it is like no salon I have been in before; no women, except the Princess; no Junkers save her and Metternich. Metternich circles among his guests, stopping for a few words; in the main he asks questions, and it is apparent that he is probing for information about the state of government – the running of the treasury, or the amount of information coming from Pest, in Hungary; before long, however, he has returned to his chair, and the officials are left to converse with sufficient brio as not to make it obvious they are listening to his conversation with the Princess.

Metternich is a notorious womaniser, and I can see that he finds the Princess attractive in spite of her age; and I suppose there is something in her lack of inhibition, besides her magnificent hair, that makes her so. He is quick to suggest how pleased the Count must be to have her company, and to ask if she finds any difference in the Rasumovsky palace. 'I sometimes think,' he adds, 'that the Count and his father here,' – he smiles indulgently at Peter Andreyich, whose face is a perfect blank – 'brought more treasure with them out of Italy than Bonaparte himself! But I have heard of no new additions. He has, however, acquired our best musicians. No doubt you will be treated to some string quartets.'

'My dear Prince,' replies the Princess, 'I hope that I can be of assistance to my brother-in-law. Of course, he is despondent that Russia feels obliged to maintain its peace with France. As to the palace itself, I should like to see some changes. Busy men, you know, are apt to be lax with their servants. I do not entirely approve of this quartet as a permanent thing, if they are to be part of the establishment, for only Herr Mayseder there is wholly presentable.'

'Indeed,' says Metternich, 'we have so many musicians these days that I was surprised he did not choose some better-looking ones. But I suppose that these are considered best at playing the works of Beethoven? Speaking of servants, I have lent the Count a strong and capable fellow, though, I admit, not handsome either. In our current circumstances I felt that you would find a strong coachman reassuring.'

'Beethoven!' exclaims the Princess. 'That is just what I mean – his presence is unnecessary! No-one disputes his genius – but let him be paid and not be seen!'

'Personally,' says Metternich, 'I find his music as inharmonious as he is indecorous. I regret that the Archduke admires him so excessively.'

At this moment Peter Andreyich, whom I had thought understood nothing, since they are speaking in French, firmly shakes his head. Metternich notices, but does not react, except by turning his head more towards the Princess.

'As you know,' he adds, 'Beethoven is a German, not a citizen. You must let me know if either he or these musicians, two of whom are also foreign, cause you to have any concern.'

I retreat, with caution, out of earshot, and sit down with my fiddle against the wall. Perhaps, I think, I can make a show of testing the strings. The bony, dangerous-looking man sits down beside me.

'Interesting conversation.' I look at him in surprise. 'You see,' he adds, looking across to Zmeskall and Carl Beethoven, 'a hint has been purposely dropped to the composer's friends, so they may rein him in. But I am pleased to meet you, Herr Mayseder. I have bought your father's wine – and have sold it to Prince Metternich. He knows good wine better than he knows good music. Your father's wine has gone to my brother in England too, where I once heard Georg Friedrich Handel. You have heard of him?' I shake my head. ' Now,' he continues slyly, 'although I *do* like Beethoven at times, it is true that he is too wild. Handel and Haydn have more poise.'

Thinking of this afternoon and Beethoven's new quartet I shake my head. That had poise, and more. But who is this man?

'In my opinion,' I say slowly, for I have only just thought it, 'he is far greater than Haydn. His music – the symphonies – reflect our troubled times.'

'Ah,' he says, 'you are young. But be wise! A composer like you might do as well as Haydn; better, if like Beethoven, he is not any one Prince's dependent – that I do admire. If I can be of assistance to you, let me know.'

'And who *are* you?' I ask.

'Salomon Rothschild, banker.'

I play my waltzes, but no-one dances. I play the anthem from Haydn's Emperor Quartet, knowing that it must be greeted with approval. Haydn himself is dying, now, in Vienna: they say that he plays that anthem to himself. The pock-marked coachman comes into the room, which seems a little odd, especially when I see him exchange a look with Metternich. Of course, he is Metternich's man, a spy. More oddly still it is this coachman who later hands me a purse from the Prince. I find I have been lavishly paid.

***

Fritz is asleep when I return. The image of Therese Linke rises before me again, and once more I put it aside. I slide into my own bed and dream I am in the castle again, and dream all the ladies have now come back from their spas – the little girls in satin, and the women pomaded, jewelled, with naked breasts and throats. I dream that I take an axe and their clothes fall off, and then I lop them limb by limb, until the blood flows everywhere. Then one more woman comes towards me, completely naked, with her hair coiled down and her marble breasts thrust out.

When I wake it is still half-dark. Fritz is lying still, with his head under the blankcts. I gct up quietly, open the window, looking towards the city, and then down at the glass roof of the Canova room. Beneath it the statues stand like ghosts. I look down to my right and see Princess Lichnowsky, looking out from her window in the other wing. Her dark mane hangs in the breeze and, within her dressing-gown, her narrow breasts are half-exposed.

There's a rattle of wheels below, and then the thud-thud-thud of running, booted feet. An open calèche appears with armed men running beside it on either side. A man is lying in it; a Frenchman, I guess, of distinction, though I can make out nothing more than a pale, oval face. Suddenly he lets out a piercing, inhuman scream; and as the carriage rattles and turns he pulls his own blanket aside and I see that one of his legs is gone. The Princess looks up, and sees me above her. Her face is white. She bangs her window shut.

A moment later I see Beethoven striding away from the palace. It is obvious that he is deep in thought. I can see the sheets of music from yesterday poking from his tail-coat pocket. I run out, down the stairs, through the silent palace, past the porter, down the steps and up the street until I am walking beside him, gulping air. He takes no notice of me at all. I think I hear musket-fire and take him by the sleeve. He turns on me in such fury that his hat falls off and rolls.

'You!' he screams. 'Who are you?'

'You know me,' I stammer. 'Joseph Mayseder – the palace…'

He stops. He seems to think.

'Oh,' he says, '*that* place.'

'I think the French are coming back,' I tell him.

'Are they beaten?'

'I don't know.'

'They won't fire on us?' he asks, pressing his hands to his ears.

'No,' I say, 'not here; but we should avoid them.'

He nods grimly, and then a slow smile comes across his face. The street is empty again, and quiet. He bends down and retrieves his hat; then he holds out his hand.

'You must visit me, young man. Bring your fiddle, when you have time. As for the French, they can't take *this* – and as for that palace, let it burn!' He taps his forehead and hums a tune as he turns off towards his lodgings.

I return, exhausted, to my father's house, where I eat and then sleep.

4. Schuppanzigh: (4th July, 1810)

I have been told the Count will see me in the library. It is the day of Princess Lichnowsky's ball; but the Count, Princess or no (and she has made her disapproval plain), will retain his custom of chamber music after supper. So I wait this morning, in my respectful attitude, feeling, as always, faintly ridiculous. Respect, however, is what is required – more so it seems than in the past. Now that the war is completely over, Bonaparte gone home to Paris with his Hapsburg bride, and normal order restored in the city, Rasumovsky the Russian must embrace the decorum that wounded Austrian pride requires. Beethoven must keep calling hours, and Sophie Weiss must not be seen. The Count must curtail himself, and therefore so must we. I wear my livery most of the time, and move about the palace discreetly. Respect is in the air.

There is, at least, plenty of music. After their absence last summer when the French were in town, the Junkers are making the most of Vienna; and the Court, of course, are recovering from the shock of seeing Arch-Duchess Marie-Louise morganatically wedded to the Emperor of the French; only after, it is rumoured, he failed to marry a Russian princess. Some of those around our Empress blame Metternich for persuading our Emperor to agree; but from Spain to Russia Bonaparte is Master of Europe. There was little choice. So there is plenty of music to distract us all, here or with Lobkowitz, and in the Schwarzenberg gardens. This ball at Count Rasumovsky's will mark the end of the season.

Our music stands and chairs in one corner remind me of our late-night soirées when this room is another place – a candle-lit troll-cave filled with sounds that seem as unearthly as Prospero's isle. This is the strange, private return on his old investment that the Count extracts from us: Beethoven, always Beethoven, in an unending exploration taking place in front of those three – the Count in his Turkish robe, beneath which he is naked; Sophie in her satin dress; Peter Andreyich, all ears. No word is ever exchanged. Peter Andreyich hears precisely, every sound of every string. Sophie sits like a mock-Hapsburg, with a fold below her chin. I do not know what she hears: only that her green eyes glitter. The good Count sits between them. He is half-relaxed, and yet nothing of the sort. He makes me think of a red-eyed fakir, drugged upon his bed of nails.

As I stand here this morning waiting for him to come in and discuss the concert, I can hear a woman's cry. It sounds odd in this clear light.

Every time we play we are in another world; I and Linke, Weiss and Mayseder. Beethoven's men - the Count's men, willed by him to wrest some further secret from these three quartets which are linked to his name: something within it that we have yet to find. (There's that woman's cry again!) For each of us the music goes deeper – into our souls I would say, but differently for each. It leavens Linke's earthiness, even as he loves to delve. It makes Weiss skip, and forget he is anxious – even to forget that his wife is entangled with the Count. It makes young Mayseder smile in spite of himself, and lean to me more trustingly, letting me lead him, showing him how to really respond. Time stands still – a tableau vivant. Josef Mayseder rooms, sometimes, with the new little page, two pretty ones together, both fair; but the one who attracts me, now and then, (it would be like touching a spring) is this curly-headed boy-composer Mayseder – especially when I catch a sight of the light brown down on his chin. What he and that page-boy do together (I am sure they do) is another little play I'd like to watch! But somewhere, right now, a woman screams, and the Count has forgotten me. That woman is in pain. A fight perhaps, or a girl in childbirth? My Mechthilt cried out like that: but then our child died, like Weiss's. The sunlight shines on a wall of books. Bigot, the French librarian, has gone home to Paris too. The cry which draws my ear comes from high among those shelves. A balcony runs across them, wrought in Polish iron from the shores of the Baltic, and in the corner, going up, a stocking of a staircase – as transparent, neglected, aspiring, as Marie

Walewska herself. Mounting it, however, does not prove so easy. I suppose I may be called fat – Falstaffian, as my Lord Beethoven says. At the first turn of the steps I am gripped, as if the dainty iron is an instrument of torture. I remember my hatred of being off the ground. Even ascending the great palace stairs makes me feel unsafe; I am always afraid of fire, and besides, to make music one must be grounded. With a mighty, despairing heave, holding my fiddle before me, I reach the turn where there is a platform, and there I pause for breath.

I knew La Walewska was doomed last year when we played one of Beethoven's sonatas, of which, it seemed, Bonaparte had heard. The piano sounded troubled, the violin in pain, and I felt sorry for her, that day at Schonnbrunn, as she sat there with the French Emperor, and his child in her belly, while he was planning how to send her away. I looked little at Bonaparte. He seemed effaced, washed out. Nor was he a patch on my Count, though fully and equally restless. Bonaparte was an artillery captain; Count Rasumovsky was trained in the English navy, and even now he has the roll of a sailor on land. The only thing Bonaparte has, which the Count has not, is his Corsican killer's instinct, which I do not rate. The Count of course arranged it and took us there - Russian diplomacy, either for or against the Polish woman, with or without the connivance of Metternich. How he really felt about it all I could not say.

I climb another stair. I climb on, I overcome. The woman screams and here I am, up on the balcony, looking through the windows into the street. Madame Bigot played piano on that occasion. I suppose because she is French. And she didn't talk: never said a word. I might have seen her on this balcony once, helping perhaps to catalogue the books. Beethoven was almost distraught when she left – woman's company soothes him, and he often needs soothing. The Bigots are back in Paris now, in time for the nuptials of Napoleon of France, and Princess Marie-Louise, of the Hapsburg House of Austria and the Holy Roman Empire. Marie Walewska, the Polish mistress, is back in Cracow.

The woman screams again – nearer now, but quieter too. A diminuendo. Funny how I never give up, in spite of my cowardice. She might after all be playing at screaming, it's hard to tell; but certainly these books are playing at books. The Works of Aristotle are cunningly painted on leather, and here, between the rows, there's a handle. The door opens outward, and behind it there's another one of green baize. It opens inward on a spring as the first closes behind me, and I see the Count.

He is in his breeches, and his torso, clear in every rib, towers before me like a Michelangelo. He holds his whip half-raised above Sophie. The backs of her sturdy thighs and her buttocks are laced with stripes of red and pink. I can see no blood. Long thin chains on her ankles attach her to the bed. From a solid brass ring in the floor another chain loops round her neck, passing through itself. The other end hangs casually upon a hook on the wall, in such a way that the whole chain, which snakes across the floor, can easily be shortened. Sophie turns her head and grins.The Count's Stradivarius lies on a small table nearby, and I guess that he seeks inspiration from his efforts.

'Schuppanzigh!' he declares, 'As you see, I am not ready to meet you quite on - equal terms. What shall we do?' He looks at Sophie, who giggles:

'Tell Schuppanzigh to undress. Then we'll be on equal terms.'

'We were about to get into bed,' says the Count, as if stating that he is off to visit Prince Kinsky, and without more words he politely shows me my place. He reads consent in my eyes.

I strip, the chains are swept away, and Sophie bounces in beside me. Then the Count pulls down his breeches and reveals his cock. I feel as if I too am bound – bound and stretched and stiff with lust. The bed has a mighty oaken frame and damask curtains. On the bedspread Europa is carried on the back of the bull. The room, unlike any other in the palace, is low-ceilinged, like a cabin, and indeed two of its windows are round like portholes. There are no other doors, and it is clearly poised somewhere between the ground floor and the first, making it as secret as it could possibly be. The air is soft and drowsy, and a green light comes from the leaves upon the trees. There are rugs on the floor and, in the window embrasure, there stands a ship's telescope.

Sophie giggles and lays her cheek on my belly. I am warm, cosy and stiff. Suddenly my cock, like a mast, is wrenched so hard to one side that I have to roll with it, rolling and plunging in Sophie's mouth while feeling the force of the Count behind her, and as he gives his great shout everything goes black and dead. It's a wonder nothing is broken! I lie there briefly, an honoured and satisfied guest, as Sophie slips back into her clothes. I see that the brass ring lifts a trap door, through which the Count hands her down, with a parting kiss. Then suddenly we both are dressed. The Count bends his magnificent frame, looks through his telescope, and utters a despairing cry. I look at him timidly.

'Beethoven!' he says, 'Beethoven everywhere! Here, man. Look for yourself.'

In the shining circle of glass, between the leaves, I can see, without doubt, Beethoven. He is no bigger than a portrait on a woman's brooch. The window where he stands is, of course, in the Birkenstock House, now the home of old Birkenstock's daughter, Antonie Brentano, wife of the merchant Franz Brentano. The place is filled to the rafters with copperplate engravings, old ash urns and Etruscan lamps, marble vases, paintings, Chinese garments, coins, sea insects, telescopes, maps and manuscripts, carved walking-sticks, and the sword of Emperor Carolus. The composer has thrown open a window and looks out, deep in thought. Now, I hardly know how, I am back in the library and Karl the ubiquitous footman , is serving us coffee.

'That fellow,' says the Count to Karl's back, 'misses nothing. I wonder what he makes of it?' I look at the Count and wonder if I can have dreamed it, so easily have we come back to the world of public duty, typified by Metternich's spy, whose barely concealed allegiance always amuses the Count. Metternich, he says, will always need him, the Russian ambassador, more than he needs Metternich. This Karl also acts as his uncle's valet, and the old man is pleased by his attentions, while he is the only person for whom Karl seems to feel a genuine sympathy. Nevertheless the Count gets up to see that no-one is listening outside the door. 'Our composer,' he says, looking at me fixedly, 'has reached his peak, I think, in Vienna.'

I nod my head, wondering. Six symphonies, each more wondrous than the last. Too many sonatas to count. A handful of string quartets. Five piano concertos. But his peak? Who knows?

'And of course,' the Count continues, 'he still talks of going to Kassel, of all places….the ludicrous court of that ludicrous younger Bonaparte. Why are you smiling?'

'Sire,' I say, 'it is all talk. He will not leave Vienna.'

'By God, Schuppanzigh,' snaps the Count, 'he can and will – but not for Kassel. Can you guess where to, I wonder?'

Lobkowitz, Rudolph and Kinsky. At the pleading of Prince Lichnowsky (much to the horror of his Princess), those gentlemen have pledged Beethoven an income for life, if he stays in Vienna. I wondered at the time that Rasumovsky himself did not make up a fourth. A year ago Beethoven was at the palace constantly, but it seems a coolness has now arisen.

'Now,' says the Count, 'you know the Brentanos?'

I do, of course. Were we not looking just now at the Brentano-Birkenstock house? Franz Brentano, the great man of business, riding here and there, and Antonie, his wife, whom I knew before her father, Johann Melchior Birkenstock, died, back in the days when I was a pupil of Haydn. There was music-making in that same house across the Donau canal - even before the palace was built. They are people of power and wealth, and lately Beethoven has been drawn into their circle. Brentano's sister, the red-haired Bettina, has made him her pet, and Brentano has lent him money.

'He spends it like water,' says the Count, who has read my thoughts, 'and as for his promised income – the war has left the rest of them as bankrupt as Lichnowsky himself. Freedom to compose – ha-ha! And so, my dear fellow, the place for our composer is, in fact – Saint Petersburg!'

'Saint Petersburg!' I am aghast. Saint Petersburg, where the blood freezes, and there is no wine. Surely he cannot be serious? But he looks at me with his long face balanced on that strong body, with the slightly hooded eyes from which there is no escape.

'One of the wealthiest men in Russia,' he continues, 'would like him in Saint Petersburg. He will receive an annuity, paid in gold, guaranteed against inflation, higher than any offer he has had before. Von Goethe himself will assist, for Weimar appreciates Russia. It also borrows from Russia. And for Beethoven, will this not be for him as an Italian Journey? His talent will *flourish* in Petersburg.'

'Your Highness,' I say quietly, 'the Archduke loves Beethoven. Surely he will not let him leave?'

'Ha!' retorts the Count. 'We *all* love Beethoven: but, does he love us? Is he not a prey to agitators? Does he not still, at just the wrong time, speak out against Bonaparte? Is he not sympathetic to Walewska and the Poles? Does he not sell his music to England, the common enemy? Is he not disrespectful to my esteemed Prince Metternich, who would approve of such a - garnish - to our friend's career?'

He pauses for effect. The light, high up, picks out the spines of books in Russian, Italian, French, and the works of Aristotle. There is a faint rustle outside: the sound of other callers and all the intricate workings of this house. The Count takes a look at his watch.

'He will be safer in Petersburg,' he says calmly. 'All I ask is that you encourage him. Tell him how much he'll be paid. And when the time comes, you can go with him. The Rasumovsky quartet will ensure his fame there, as well as mine! In return, Schuppanzigh, I will get you concerts *both* here and there. You will be a very rich man!'

I've said he has no killer's instinct. It is sheer restless energy in that long nose, those perfect limbs.

'But who will look after him?' I ask. Who indeed, with no Streichers, no Sophie, no Zmeskall, no Stefan Breuning; nor even his brother, nor Countess Erdody, nor his pupil the Archduke. 'Why, his future wife of course. Young Fraulein

Brentano, the honourable merchant's sister, with whom he is – intimate. She will marry genius, providing it has wealth. It is simple, Schuppanzigh. I will dazzle her with St Petersburg tonight. You do the same with Beethoven. Here,' and he tosses it into my lap, 'is a book to help you.'

I take a deep breath. St Petersburg! It seems insane, but then when great men use their power, the insane happens quite often.

'I will try then Sire,' I say, 'but – Madame Weiss will miss him.'

The Count looks upwards and stretches out his legs. I seem to see every hair on his head and every neat button on his frock-coat. Suddenly the elegant fingers, which yet remind me of claws, bunch themselves into fists.

'Sophie,' he says, 'makes too much of him; and she confides in him, what she should not. I must have *her* to myself.'

***

Following the usual instructions about this evening – Haydn's 'Emperor' (something they might recognise), and the first of Opus 59 – and our liveries to be fresh, and Linke to give it vibrato – I am walking away through the city, as so often before, wondering what to make of him; and what it would be like, after all, if that colossal palace had never come into being. St Stephen's rises above me: Vienna both of solid stone and rickety wooden garrets; and in it the burghers, waggons, whores, taverns, musicians and priests. I would go to my Mechthilt, if only I were not so restless! I actually pass our house and carry on. At the Theater-An-Der-Wien I remember something else of Beethoven's – *Leonore*. I'd forgotten. The young wife who dresses herself as a page-boy in order to rescue her husband. Six symphonies, one opera. But, of course, everyone else has forgotten that opera too. I hum myself the overture as I head for the Schwan.

It reminds me of one strange night last summer, in the war, when the Count disparaged this opera to that Frenchman, the Capitaine, and the Frenchman would not have it. There were only the four of us, alone in the library. The Count was in his cups, Sophie was pregnant with his child, and this Frenchman,

Ramballe, was defending *Leonore*, sometimes called *Fidelio*. He had heard it back in '05, when we gave the French the keys and had a more friendly occupation: the year of Austerlitz. He seemed to be merely a soldier, this man, but I do not pretend to know the workings of diplomacy. Perhaps he was simply agreeable. He showed Sophie great respect, and, it seemed, had once known Linke's brother's wife and her daughter. Hearing this, the Count had declared that if he were in Linke's place he would marry that woman. The Frenchman looked at him and Sophie. His look expressed precisely that they were sitting together like man and wife.

'Ah, my friend,' the Count exclaimed, 'only an Emperor, and a French one too, can marry as he likes!'

'Besides which, Captain,' added Sophie, 'I am married already. And no Anna Linke is going to take my husband!' This I could make no sense of. This Anna, Linke's demi-spouse, never comes near the palace. She is a dressmaker. But then Sophie's jealousies often defy all reason. For she is jealous of Weiss when she is not faithful to him…or say that when she is with him she is, and when she is with the Count, she is faithful to *him*.

I was called upon to give my talk about Beethoven, in which I presented the Opus 59 as his crowning achievement to date. Ramballe was quite entranced. Sophie and the Count warbled snatches of some theme, which I gave them back again upon the violin. Then I played them gypsy dances.

'And I know, I know,' sang Sophie, 'where that Anna Linke lives.'

It seemed they had agreed, in passing, that the Captain should call on her. She should have a surprise – and Linke should not know.

'But, my dear fellow,' the Count had said, 'that opera shows the weakness of the man. It is not myth, like Mozart or Shakespeare, nor is it funny, or true to life. Beethoven cannot make us believe that a grown woman disguises herself as a boy, nor indeed that freedom comes merely from being brave. We have sans-culottes now, not Leonores.'

'All the same,' Sophie remarked, 'they tried to suppress it, did they not?'

The Count smiled. 'Ah, the Austrian government! Simply because we are shown a man imprisoned without trial… But who is Fidelio? What does he or she achieve? It's not clear.'

Ramballe pulled on his moustaches and drew his bushy brows together.

'I beg to differ!' he exclaimed. 'The triumph of love is always fine. There is chivalry and honour. There is the mad courage of woman. What can be more universelle? There may still be Leonores, as there are still black tyrants.'

It strikes me now, as I walk, and feel the heat of the cobbles, that it was Sophie herself, her courage, that Ramballe had in mind. I could see he was drawn to her. These soldiers lead a lonely life. It was that brief time last year during the occupation, but before the Princess arrived, when the Count displayed her like a wife, and she does have a mad courage, as well as her motherly side. In some ways she is not unlike Mechthilt, only I think more afraid to be alone. It was a pity her child died, like ours, though I suppose it was not intended, and she and Weiss have a boy, the one who is with Lichnowsky at Gratz. Feeling sorry for all of us, I make my way to the Schwan.

Did I know he'd be in here; with Zmeskall, of course, the old know-all? Drinking wine already. That was an odd thing, seeing him in the Brentano house. Not because of the Count and the telescope; just because he always works in the morning. And I still have this book! Well, I'm not ready to tackle him yet, if I ever am. As I eat my schnitzel I think again of Mechthilt: wrestling; getting astride her; sharing a piece of cake; boxing my weary brain inside her colossal breasts. We are fat people. Do we care? My fat person is split in two halves: flesh and spirit; traitor and friend.

I'm leaving when he catches my eye. A finger beckons.

'I have something for *you*,' he growls. 'Or rather, Zmeskall has.'

I bow politely to Count Nikolaus Zmeskall von Domanovecz, Imperial Court Secretary, and a man who makes the cello groan aloud. He looks at me and shrugs with his pleasant, wrinkled smile.

'What have we for my Lord?' he asks.

'For My Lord Falstaff? Ha, ha, ha!' Beethoven tugs at his tail pocket until a thick and stained roll of paper appears. A manuscript! I put my hand out eagerly.

'Attendez, Falstaff! Sit down. No, get me a quill.' Quill and ink are added to the drops of tallow, dust and scraps of food. He clears a space with his paw and flattens out the paper. He speaks aloud, but as to himself:

'Dedié a mon *vrai* ami – the old scamp Zmeskall. *Quartetto Serioso.*' He looks up and thrusts it across, reaching out for the wine which Zmeskall has thoughtfully moved to the table end.

'It's his, but you might play it for him at one of your Thursdays. Get to know it. On condition.'

'On condition what?'

'Don't show it to that wretched Count.'

'Rasumovsky?' I seem surprised. 'I thought he was your favourite?'

'Did you? Well he's not!'

'You know,' I say, with sudden inspiration, 'he knows of someone who would pay a king's ransom to have you in St Petersburg – but, of course, it would kill him if you left. You're not meant to hear of it.'

'*Where* did you say?' He turns his better ear.

'St Pe-ters-burg.'

'Ha! The Russian wilderness! Forget it, Schuppanzigh.'

'Oh,' I say, 'but it was not my – '

'And,' Zmeskall interrupts, 'there is your *contract* with the princes.'

The Master shoots him a look. It must be the only undiplomatic thing Zmeskall's ever said, but of course *he* is terrified of losing him. He knows he will go down to posterity as Beethoven's friend. He is, by good chance, easy to lip-read, with his mincing mouth.

'Well,' says Beethoven, 'of course I wouldn't go, certainly not now…but I'd like to know how much.' It is my turn to shrug.

'These Russians,' I say. 'They don't know what money is. Look at our Count now. Where does it all come from?'

'Serfs,' he says abruptly, and turns his chair to one side.
***

It seems that before I have time to draw breath I am back in the palace, my fiddle under my arm, as it has been nearly all day. Every surprise these days seems to fade rapidly into the daily round. I remember the Count saying something similar to Ramballe: that one thing he liked in the opera was just the word 'Augenblick'. 'What a moment!' But, he said, he always felt, in his own life, or in today's world, as if that one special moment, that 'Augenblick', would never arrive. Yet he has everything.

We rehearse, again, in the library. Is it the same place as this morning? I spend more time on the Haydn, although they know it well enough. The new boy, Fritz, has put out our copies, and for some reason Mayseder and Linke both keep glancing at him. Afterwards I stay in the palace and take my rest upstairs in the attic. I will see Mechthilt tomorrow. I could have gone for a bite with Weiss, who asked me, wanting as always to talk about Beethoven; but I do not want to do that, nor do I find his little cottage peaceful. I am pleased for him, though, because his flame-haired son is back. The Lichnowskys have brought him on their visit before they return to Gratz. For the next two months Vienna will slumber in the heat. The Junkers who can afford it will go to the spas, while Beethoven will take rooms in one of the villages. I will remain to organise the weekly outdoor concerts which the court officials and the burghers will attend. There will be just enough musicians to make them go.

My little room is like a cell. I have done the penance of four flights of stairs. Now, until the ball begins, everything is close to peace. The workings of the palace below are no more than a muffled throb. Before I lie down to rest I look from the narrow window. There is the terrace below, a few rose-bushes and an English yew-maze. The little cottage with its fence is at one side, near the ballroom, set in the orchard where apples and pears are starting to swell. Half-hidden behind them is a fairly low brick wall, and behind that the canal, up which the Count's goods, his furniture, his statues, his blocks of masonry and his paintings were towed a few years ago. The wealthiest man in Europe, people said. The Birkenstock house is there, just as it was this morning. Perhaps the Count is right. Beethoven will marry the young red-headed Bettina Brentano, with her never-ending allusions to her dear friend Goethe. And then, after all, who knows? A wife can do a good deal. Only last month he wanted to marry one of his pupils, but she cared more for her little dog. Marriage is never far from his mind. But, I ask myself, how can he, Beethoven, be happy? It's not in his nature, is it? Or do I not know him as well as I think? And suddenly I remember the manuscript in my pocket. In the long pocket in the coat that hangs on the back of the door! I seize it and begin to read. 'Quartetto Serioso, dedié à Zmeskall': something wrong with that. There was another look in his eye when he gave it me. I remember six years ago, when he was getting over the Guiccardi girl, and we all went to Zmeskall's favourite whorehouse. I still remember that slender, brown-eyed brunette who boasted a roman nose between her long ringletted hair; flat in the chest but wide in the hips, who, in spite of the gaps in her teeth, had that knack of looking so expressionless that one believed she was unaware and, indeed, far beyond, the use to which her body was put; but he gazed eagerly into her eyes. So yes, he's always in love, but never quite right for it: Madame Bigot another one. Then a sonata: 'Les Adieux'. I read through the bars: stop, read them again; read them forwards, backwards. My head is beginning to spin. This man is gloriously in love! Or so I read it. Can I be wrong? Of course, this is no ordinary love. It begins like a whirlwind. Then it sets the teeth on edge. Even in the finale it is dancing on a precipice. Yes, there are only two voices. Four instruments, four dancing feet, but only two voices, two pairs of eyes. I love the dark, sidling movement: the lover, with eyes twinkling, reaches out to touch from behind…. The world, however, will find it impossible. The scholastics of the *Allgemeine Musikalische Zeitung* will pronounce him mad again. I put it down on the one wooden chair. Further thought about this or anything else will have to wait, but before I can compose myself to sleep, there's a quiet knock at the door and that strange young boy, young Fritz, enters with my red livery for the evening. I point for him to lay it on the end of the bed (there's nowhere else), and he is turning round to go, when I am struck by a thought. 'One moment,' I say. 'I hear you can play?'

He nods, a little fearfully, but not, I can tell, from doubt of his ability. We shall see about that! I pick up the score again. His eyes are a wary grey-blue, at odds with a little pout of the mouth. He needn't worry I like them older, at the selfish age when they can tumble a wench or two on the side. Besides, I have given up the habit of falling in love with younger men. I pass him my fiddle, and hold up the sheets of paper, smoothing them against my chest.

'Play this,' I say. 'But – mind – it's a secret. You're not to tell *anyone* – understood?'

He nods, and I feel I can trust him. I watch his thin arm heft.

At first I'm disappointed. The opening bars, that burst of starlight, come out like a horse and cart. I'm shaking my head, enough, when suddenly he finds a weeping, unearthly, abandoned dance of desire, of joy and foreknowledge of loss, that I had only half-heard. Then, suddenly, he stops. I have forgotten to turn the page! He looks up, waiting, but not as I would be waiting, and at that moment I grasp the truth: the puzzle of his isolation, the way that others glance at him when they think I'm not looking. This boy is in fact a girl! And I can see she knows I know – impudent little miss! 'Thank-you,' I say, taking back my fiddle - and then, as she turns away a little wearily, as do all those who spend whole nights and days in the palace, I add: 'My dear boy, you *are* a musician!' He does not turn, but a wag of the head shows he is grinning – like a boy.

I cannot stop to wonder about her either. I am soon descending, in my scarlet livery, by wooden and by marble stairs, into the golden workings of Princess Lichnowsky's ball. In the Canova room I nibble at the dishes set for those not dining formally: quails with caviar; pheasants stuffed with chestnut; pastries, tarts and Alpine cheese. After the concert we will all go down into the kitchen to eat, and pinch the wenches' bottoms. Linke will carry one off. Because he's lame, poor fellow. But he has a way.

Sophie comes up to me smiling, dressed in her best white smock. She sent the boy. She knows. She looks with approval at the clothes she has altered.

'Come along with me, Ignaz.'

She leads me through the Canova room, up the narrow stair in the corner, whence a blind corridor leads us back on ourselves. It occurs to me that somewhere on our journey we have passed the Count's low-ceilinged, secret bedroom. We take each other's hands, for we are both suddenly tired to death; but hearing the cacophonous tuning-up of the orchestra in the distance, we smile in spite of ourselves. We pass a door that must connect with the first-floor apartments, and we are in a high gallery, with the sky-blue ceiling just above our heads, and before us a chandelier whose candles blink in our faces and send out a whiff of wax. We are looking down on the ballroom, observing but unobserved.

The orchestra is a dozen or so, the Karnthenor's second fiddles, along with that same young boy or girl, and joking with him now is Weiss's young son on clarinet. He is red-haired, fresh-faced, freckled and suddenly tall. Truly, his hair seems to burn under the glow of the candles. I am about to ask his name when I remember it: Hans.

Sophie's eyes observe them both with care, then move to Princess Lichnowsky. I think of how it was different, not so many years ago: Francis still reigning as Holy Roman Emperor; the Junkers at their ease; Beethoven suddenly composing the Eroica; Prince and Princess Lichnowsky in their town-house, living and breathing music. Then the battle of Austerlitz, and Countess Rasumovsky died, and then we had our first sight of the new quartets. Everything became less certain. Beethoven (who of course is not here) seems to have got beyond us all once more. At one time I thought that he was also in love with Sophie, but I see now that he longs for something more ethereal. Perhaps he really will marry La Brentano. Sophie's hand is still in mine as we watch the Princess below us greeting her guests, with the Count upright at her side. Neither of us is required until the chamber concert after the supper – if the Princess had her way we would not be required at all. While the Lichnowskys are staying every servant must always be in his or her expected place. The Princess is the keeper of her dead sister's memory. As for Sophie, the Count keeps her hidden and the Princess tries to ignore this liaison, of which she is fully aware. In her odd, excitable way the Princess looks the Grande Dame now, in her scarlet dress, her narrow embonpoint polished and lifted beneath those high, wide shoulders, topped with the tresses of her unpredictable head.

Among her guests (that is, the Count's) are the Archduke Rudolph and our Emperor Francis, with his wife; Prince Metternich and secretary Gentz; Countess Maria Erdody, feathered like a little wren; Princess Bagration, wife of the Russian general; Bilibin, a Russian diplomat; Jerome Bonaparte, King of Westphalia, the same who has offered Beethoven a position in Kassel; the Princes Lobkowitz and Kinsky; Franz Brentano, a merchant, with his wife Antonie, and his red-haired sister Bettina. Present, but not announced, is Prince Lichnowsky, the husband, wearing a green frock-coat of a certain age.

I turn back to the orchestra. Linke and Weiss have been roped in, while Mayseder, young and debonair, conducts. After the Emperor and Empress, younger couples dance to a fairly tasteful selection of old tunes – even one of Beethoven's old, lovely variations on Mozart – marred, before too long, by Mayseder's 'Princess Polka'. I look again at the girl disguised as a boy, and think that this must be Linke's gifted niece who, now I think of it, he has ceased to mention. The memory of Captain Ramballe, the mention of Anna Linke that I recalled today: there is some dull mystery there.

Now Rasumovsky waltzes with golden-haired Bettina Brentano, who is wearing sky-blue silk. Then he leads out the Princess. He is dazzling white, upright, against her scarlet and black. The other guests applaud. Sophie beside me bursts into tears.

Mayseder is still glowing with pride when, after supper, we

mount the musicians' platform. Weiss is there already. I don't think he has moved. A few young ladies in ball-gowns, with a few young officers and gentlemen, shuffle back, disappointed to see the chairs set out. They, of course, would prefer more dancing. I see young 'King Jerome' among them, preening himself. It's hard to believe that he has offered the Master a salary, and harder still to believe that it was he who carried out the siege of Breslau, when Weiss's father was killed. In Vienna we felt the French cannonade and promptly surrendered, but Breslau was bombarded until the walls were turned to rubble. The fellow Karl is holding a tray, from which Prince Metternich takes a fluted stem in his long, polished fingers, and they exchange a glance. I realise now that I have made a mistake. We should be playing the Haydn last, in honour of the Emperor; great Haydn who is dead. My heart, however, says there is only one right order: Beethoven's work has the largest scope; and it's not as if many will be listening. Once they are finally seated the Haydn goes well, until we have a distraction, as Peter Andreyich appears from somewhere, clattering in his bony way across the polished floor. Heads are turned in execration; but then, seeing who it is, most of them, led by the Princess, compose looks of respectful indulgence. When we finish there is polite applause, and brutal clapping from a few who have had to have the anthem explained to them: '*Autriche uber alles*'. Indeed. Peter Andreyich has now joined Prince Metternich and Karl; all three of them stiff and stark as dolls as the audience stretch their legs and more champagne is served. The old man looks up trustingly at Karl, who has his back towards me and seems to be interpreting. I wonder if Peter Andreyich knows any German or French. Count Rasumovsky throws him a smiling glance as he makes himself agreeable to the Emperor and Empress. Archduke Rudolph, young, sweating and bald, turns in his seat to Prince Lichnowsky.

'I look forward to the Beethoven,' says one. 'It has not been much played.'

'Ah, Beethoven!' replies the other.

'Ah, Beethoven!' is Rudolph's reply.

Antonie and Franz Brentano, sitting very still among the nodding heads, listen to their exchange. Meanwhile Bettina Brentano is talking to Princess Lichnowsky: 'A wonderful man your highness – no respecter of rank, but so droll. And so tender! Would you believe that when my belle-soeur Antonie – that is she, I'm sure you know her – when she was terribly ill he came and improvised quietly in the next room. For three hours, was it not? And then, without a word, he left. Leaving just the music you see, for music heals without our knowledge, whereas, as my friend Goethe says, with words the reader must find his own cure…'

I wonder if Bettina has yet received a book on the many wonders of St Petersburg. Sophie comes up, limping, with more glasses of wine and, for a moment, the Emperor smiles. Every guest, with a few exceptions, becomes attached to her; for even as she twinkles with feminine mischief she is also, to some of their eyes, the ideal subject: the clean, mannerly peasant-woman making her obeisance. But from across the room, where Karl is serving, the old man frowns at her and the Princess, who is talking to Metternich (I hear 'Beethoven' uttered in disdainful tones) follows his look and scowls. Suddenly Peter Andreyich bows. One expects him to snap in half. But who is he bowing to? The Princess looks at him fondly; but I see his eyes are fixed, if fixed they are at all, on Antonie Brentano, who has chanced to look that way. She has one of those oval faces, not unlike Sophie's, but smoother, and capped with a higher, squarer brow, so that her big, dark eyes appear, when her face is tilted up, like dark pools tinged with moonlight. There is, at any rate, a strange light in them as she looks at Peter Andreyich, and he stares rheumily back. As I watch it occurs to me that Peter Andreyich, above all, would miss Beethoven if he were really to go to St Petersburg; he, along with Lichnowsky and the Archduke. It may be only this music that keeps the old man alive. I am still watching as we tune up. Let us play Opus 59, number 1, and see what their faces reveal. First I have to be sure that we are playing together: young Mayseder, battling fairly to do it justice; Linke glad to drive his bow; Weiss unfolding and folding, always finding something new. Now I look at the audience. There are the usual few rapt expressions dotted among bored looks: Peter Andreyich watching as ever; the Count looking down at his feet. Princess Lichnowsky's mouth is open in surprise. Perhaps she has not truly heard it before.

I am looking more and more at the woman in the dark blue dress: Antonie Birkenstock-Brentano. She is looking intently at us; but this is not Peter Andreyich's hard stare. Surrounded by sequins, medals, tiaras, she is like one of those dusty, faint objects roaming the starlit sky. Between her sandy-haired husband and her golden sister-in-law she is even less visible. She wants to be invisible, but tonight she alone is the one who is living the music and giving it back to me. I think of the new quartet lying in my attic, and hope that one day I shall play it for her. Someone else, Metternich, has noticed her absorption. He is still standing and gives her a critical look. One might really say that we are haunted by the absent composer; but, as we reach our climax, Metternich is distracted by a messenger. Crow-like he tiptoes across to his Emperor. The two men walk aside while we are applauded. Then our Emperor Francis walks out before us stiffly, and holds up his hand. He makes the announcement in his toneless Hapsburg voice: 'With regret I have to inform you of the death of Princess Schwarzenburg. We understand that she was killed in a fire, in Paris, at our embassy.'

He pauses, has finished. Metternich speaks in his ear.

'The fire was at a ball, in celebration of – the nuptials of our - niece, and the French – Emperor. Our niece – is not harmed.'

All react with sudden shock, which mutates to a vast sigh. It is a great dying chord. The Emperor looks slowly around. Metternich is still at his ear.

'We thank the Count Rasumovsky, for his hospitality. We shall be pleased to hear again the last bit – the, ah, '*thème Russe*' – from this piece, and then depart.' This means an early finish for us. No late-night mazurkas for those who still desire to dance. I give the cue, and as we play I look at their faces; noble, savage, crooked or bland. In their eyes I see the licking of flames at curtains, the fire running wild through carpets, the cracking of great gilt mirrors. Portraits melt in their frames, bodies tumble down stairs and chandeliers crash to the floor. Ball-gowns turn to ash. Flesh melts, bones char. I am afraid of fire. I know how quickly it spreads. I know how a man like me might easily be trapped, and exactly how my flesh would roast inside my clothes. It is my fear that sooner or later, at some late night concert like this, a candle will overturn and we shall be on fire.

I also see all their suppressed hatred of Bonaparte; ambivalence to Metternich; respect for the young Tsar, who refused to give his sister to the Corsican. The jaunty tune is a song of hate. They hate the French and some of them also hate the Count. Some even hate Beethoven. They want a day of reckoning.

Only when this *Allegro* slows and becomes, by some miracle, thoughtful, does Antonie, Madame Brentano, draw me back to her, hearing it both as we play it and in her own special way, and suddenly I understand what my heart, and that new quartet, have already told me: Count Rasumovsky's mistake.

Beethoven cannot marry Bettina, the sister. He is in love with the wife.

Second Quartet: Summer 1812
5. Weiss

It is three years since my wife miscarried, three since Hans was sent away, and two since I saw him last, back in the summer of 1810. It is six years since I came here from Breslau, with my wife and Josef Linke. It is three since the French were here, who are now for Russia. It is Russia's turn to suffer, and it is said that Bonaparte is sending the biggest army there that the world has ever known. Three years ago Russia was friends with France; now it is Austria who is her ally, and we are even sending some regiments to fight with the French against the Russians. I ask Sophie what the Count thinks. 'He thinks it is unfortunate' she says.

So time has passed and yet, for me, it has stood quite still. I have ceased to think about Breslau so I suppose I have become a Viennese. I never leave the city. I spend my time studying, trying to improve my playing. I practise with Schuppanzigh, when he has the time. With the Count's permission I have played in the orchestras; I have been able to take a part in the Seventh Symphony, and in the new music for Egmont. At Lobkowitz's palace we performed the new quartet, which Schuppanzigh agreed with me in calling 'The Harp'. Schuppanzigh has mysteriously promised that there will be another quartet, this year. Beethoven has only to decide when and how he wants it performed. Then there have been similar, intimate concerts here, for the cognoscenti, in which the Count always has one or another of Opus 59. And every few months, still, we play to him in private, and Sophie sits beside him. I should like to ask her about her feelings, as she hears the second over again, as Peter Andreyich still watches and watches, and the Count and we wrestle with its ever-changing shape; but afterwards, in our cottage, I never know how to begin. Otherwise, when we are together, we are as we always were, although it is different now that Hans is gone. She likes to have my arm around her and feel safe, just the way she did when we first became engaged. I don't know how she is with the Count: she goes there and returns, that's all, and we never discuss it. I suppose that, although of course the Count has been away many times, time itself has mostly stood still for them as it has for me. When she is in the palace I work in my garden, or I wander through Vienna, a free man. Once or twice I have met Anna in the marketplace. We only exchange a few words, but her affectionate smile warms me gently, like the morning sun. When I ask after Therese she tells me that she is doing well.

I go outside the cottage this morning, and begin to pull up weeds. Our daughter is still here in the corner, under her grassy mound. My thoughts drift back to Hans. How old is he now? Seventeen. How I – how we – would like to see him again.

As I'm hoeing the cabbages, Linke arrives. It is years since he called. He is there at the Count's soirées, and with me, sometimes, in the orchestras, but we hardly speak. I look at his small paunch, his wiry frame, the lame foot he carries with ease, and his grey-streaked hair. He has not really changed. I usher him inside, and fetch out my bread and cheese, my wooden cups that I brought from Breslau and my flagon of country wine. He takes off his leather hat and smiles.

'A fine hat,' I say. 'Thanks,' he says, turning it in his enormous hands, 'It belonged to my brother, once.' He is so quiet that I pick up my viola and play a few bars of the second quartet, first movement, which we will be playing this evening. More than ever this is tense, uncomfortable music. He takes a sip of wine, then suddenly holds up his hand. 'Play that again,' he says. He listens, nodding, and when I have finished he says: 'I came to tell you about the rehearsal. You know when Mayseder disappeared, the Count said he'd play second himself? Well, he's hurt his finger. The servants are saying your wife bit him, or else he cut it on a glass. I expect you know how they talk. But the point is that Fritz – the young boy, you know – will have to play second now, and so we are rehearsing again this afternoon.'

I have an unpleasant vision of Sophie with the Count. She is biting his finger, and doing other things, and I curse Linke for gossiping like an old woman, but then I see that he has something more on his mind, some trouble not of mine but of his own. The Junkers are already leaving the city for summer: some to the spas and some to their estates. Prince and Princess Lichnowsky, who have been here two months, are going back to Gratz. They did not bring Hans this time. Sophie is disappointed, but at least, this year, she does not seem to fear that Princess Lichnowsky, who becomes more and more absurd, will manage to attract the Count. We do not yet know the Count's plans – only that he is preoccupied by the coming war. The after-supper concert tonight, then, is quite a small affair. Besides the Lichnowskys there will be just a few true music-lovers: Countess Erdody, Madame Ertmann, and the Archduke, I believe; and, for the first time for many, many months, Beethoven is also invited. 'The Master will be there!' I say. 'The boy must really play well.' Linke nods. 'Indeed. Regarding the boy, though, I have a favour to ask you. You see, I am concerned about him. He cannot stay in the palace alone. If Sophie could get leave from the Count, he could spend the summer near Breslau, at Anna's parent's farm.'

I picture Anna once more. Her hair is tied in a great knot, and her arms are a little sunburned. Once I helped her carry a bale of cloth back home, but I could not accept her invitation to stay. I know which boy Linke means – he played with us on one occasion which I would rather forget, when we played the Count's composition – but he is not very sturdy. 'Perhaps,' I say, 'the Count will let him go to Prince Lichnowsky's? You know Hans is already there?'Linke shakes his head. 'Your wife has said he can go there, but she is too – busy to understand. You see, he's not – as other boys. Those bumpkins – not Hans of course– would make his life too hard.'

'There is Countess Erdody,' I say, 'I hear she is staying on. Perhaps she needs a servant ... or what about Prince Metternich?' I break off because he is staring at me in horror. I suppose he has heard things about Prince Metternich's establishment. I promise him to speak to Sophie about this farm. When he has gone I practise again, dismissing from my thoughts the business of the Count's finger, and wondering, as we all do, why Mayseder has disappeared?

***

The drowse of early afternoon has fallen on the palace now, as if there were no wars. Unable to practise more or return to my garden, I drift in through the open French windows and wander through the public rooms. Reaching the great hallway I look inside the Canova room, where Peter Andreyich is dusting the statues with a feathered stick and a rag. According to some system he moves from one to the next: Apollo, Hermes, Diana. He stoops a little to flick at their toes, then works his way up and around. He has some portable wooden steps with which, moving cautiously, he can reach their heads and breasts. Great shafts of sunlight scattered with dust encompass him and them alike. On the staircase in the far corner Sophie sits and watches him. She seems to be at her ease, and yet under some compulsion. On impulse I cross the room. Just like a dog and a cat magnetised by each other they ignore my presence. I brush on past my wife and go up, and through a blind passage, until I come out in a little secret balcony high above the ballroom. Below me Linke sits, practising with young Fritz. The blue ceiling lies over us like the sky on the Russian steppes where the towns may soon be burning. I turn and go back to where Sophie, now at the top of the stairs, holds up a warning hand.

Looking down above her head, I can see part of Peter Andreyich and two other gentlemen. One is Karl, the coachman, and the other, by his voice, and then by his yellow coat and blonde hair is, I think, Prince Metternich. He is addressing Peter Andreyich in French, but he speaks so slowly that I can understand:

'I have assured the Count,' he says, 'of my services to you, while he is away.'

Peter Andreyich bows.

'The Count does not think that Russia will make peace if Bonaparte crosses the Vilna.'

Peter Andreyich nods.'

Yet he thinks peace is possible. That they may still make friends.'

Peter Andreyich raises his duster, but does not reply.

'Of course, my dear sir, Austria is obliged to take part in this war. Bonaparte is too strong for us. But you have known the Russian court. Is it possible, do you think, that the Tsar would make peace? Or will he fight to the death?' Peter Andreyich stands impassive. He looks, unwinking, at Metternich. Then, with the ghost of a smile, he turns back to the statue of Venus, and Metternich shrugs and departs. A minute later the old man shuffles away with Karl. Sophie turns her head and smiles at me.

'What was that?' I ask. 'How should I know, except that the Count has been teasing Prince Metternich. But I have news for you: you and I will both be going to Lichnowsky at Gratz. Better still, that horrible old uncle stays here.' Linke came to see me,' I say. I repeat his request. Sophie frowns. 'That boy is trouble. No, he can't go off to Breslau. Those people of Anna's are common peasants. The Count will have him along with us, where he can fiddle away and I can keep an eye on him. Tell Josef he will be all right.'

'His playing has improved,' I say. 'Remember the Count's quartet...the one he wrote?' Sophie shoots me a glance. Perhaps it is cruel of me to remind her of that time, because I know that she thinks of the dead child often enough. She blamed herself for losing her: that was why she wanted her buried where she would see her grave every day. At the same time, of course, it was convenient. We did not have to take that little body to church and lie about the father's name. But, although this boy, this Fritz, is nothing to do with me, I do not like it when she and the Count together exert their power, as I do not like it that Prince and Princess Lichnowsky chose to leave Hans behind. I am not displeased, however, when she charges me to visit the Birkenstock House in order to remind Beethoven and the Brentanos of their invitation. She has no doubt that he will be with them this afternoon.

At one o'clock we rehearse. Schuppanzigh is dissatisfied with Fritz, asking him for a tautness he cannot muster. It is like asking the boy to catch the grimness in Beethoven's face, and at the third halt he lurches forward and grabs Fritz's instrument. Peter Andreyich, who has come to watch, makes a sudden movement. His ears turn almost black. But Ignaz addresses the boy almost caressingly: 'Like this, you see? Or, at least, as close as you can.' And, genius that he is, he plays like the boy, but adds a turn or two of his own – enough to create harmony between them. And suddenly it dawns on me that I know this boy – the elbow and shoulder are lifted up in just the way I remember - the girl upon the riverbank! The left leg jigs by itself. I look again, discreetly, so as not to frighten her. Now I have no doubt – and I understand Linke's anxiety. It is Therese Linke in disguise! Do Schuppanzigh, or Peter Andreyich, know? I remember suddenly how I talked with Anna of finding the girl a place in the palace, and then ceased to think of it. But of course – somehow - Sophie arranged it. I take another glance, hoping it will look as if I am only keeping time. The face, the short hair, will do for a boy; but the figure, I think, is changing fast, like the tip of a plant disturbing the earth. This strange discovery has happened in a flash, and in a flash I put it aside: I find myself returning deep into the music, into its torments and moments of hope, as if I had been thinking of nothing else.

***

At 98 Erdbeergasse, the famous Brentano-Birkenstock house, I wait in the hallway, looking at the engravings and the dusty porcelain plates on the walls. Pictures and other objects line the stairs: Madame Brentano is trying to get these antiquities packed and sent to museums. When I am sent up the Master is at the piano. After some minutes he glances round, smiles and stops. 'Antonie will know you are here. She'll come soon.' He nods at a door in the opposite wall. I think of his bare attic room on the Molkerbastei. The Bastion itself rises in my mind, parts of it still shattered by cannon-fire.

'And how is Madame Weiss?' He does an imitation hobble, his eyes kind and very bright. I give him her invitation. He roars: his good old roar, containing his fond memories of

Sophie, and his affectionate contempt for Lichnowsky and his mad Princess. 'I shall be delighted, for her sake and Antonie's. You know what I think of those lordlings. But Franz is not here – he left this morning.'

'Well it is only the Lichnowskys and the Count. And Countess Erdody. And the Ertmanns'

'The worse, Weiss! That *canaille* still think they own me – though of course your Rasumovsky thinks he owns everyone.'

'Are you writing, Master?'

'This and that, young Weiss. Nothing *weiss* enough for you. I need money, damn it. I have an idea: a symphony with chorus. Someone will pay for that!'

'I thought,' I say boldly, 'that the Harp was perhaps a new beginning? For a new set of quartets.'

'Plink-plink, plink-plink!' He shakes his head kindly. There *is* one more quartet though. Fatso has seen it. He'll get you to play it through soon.' So – the quartet Schuppanzigh mentioned really does exist! It had seemed too good to be true. 'At the palace?' I ask.

'Heavens, no: I wouldn't let our *diplomat* near it. In any case, I don't want to be there. You see, I wrote it just for myself. We'll see what others make of it.'

The small door opens, and Antonie Brentano quietly appears. I have seen her several times, but seeing her closer does not make her more distinct. Perhaps it's the effect of his presence. She seems like one of those brownish, nondescript birds – a nightingale perhaps.

'My Nightingale!' says Beethoven, holding out his hand. He introduces me and, turning to the window, points down, across the canal and through the trees to where my cottage sits far off in the palace grounds.

'That is a very sheltered spot!' She turns to me smiling. 'And you are a very great gardener: I have seen you.' For a moment her speech strikes me as affected; then I see that she exaggerates her lips in order to be sure that he hears. 'Well,' he says roughly, 'Rasumovsky ploughs his wife.'

This, I think, is how others see me, if they notice me at all. Even Beethoven, with his strange ménage à trois with these

Brentanos, mocks my little life. Here is this house with its treasures, over there the palace with its paintings and statues, while I cling to my wooden cups. People like Linke and I are at the mercy of these great ones: even our wives and our children are not ours. But Antonie firmly and gently ignores this last remark.

'Are you sure,' she asks him, instead, 'that you want to go to this concert? The Princess is odious. You do not need such people.' He looks astonished. No such possibility had occurred to him. 'Oh no,' he answers, 'she is only a fool. And besides, I want *us* to go together. With you beside me I am calm, and not afraid of anything!' She puts her hand in his with a lightness that startles. Their only wish, I think, is to console each other, and as I step towards the door I know that they've forgotten me. I shall see them again tonight, and it gives me some kind of hope, or courage, just to see something as natural as this; for they are as much in their own world as two nesting birds.

***

When I am dressed, and as the sun sinks, I pick up my viola and enter into the palace as quietly as a thief. I find myself once more amazed by the passage of time. How can so much change, and all this be the same?   I wonder whether, if Mayseder does not return, we shall soon forget him and find another second violin. I look around the empty ballroom. The Count and his guests are still at supper. I sit down in my place by the music-stands, and look up to the balcony I had never noticed before this morning, which makes me think of the organ-loft in our Lutheran church in Breslau. Sitting down and closing my eyes I hear the solemn music of Bach which I have left so far behind. I see myself in front of the altar, a fair-haired boy in a white smock. In the side-chapel, where my father prays, hangs the painting of Eve and the serpent; the tree-trunk with the serpent around it, and green-eyed Eve leaning towards it, giving off changing lights as if her white flesh were porcelain and yet, in her slender arms, showing all the sudden vigour that Sophie had then in hers. I open my eyes and see Fritz, alone, putting out our scores.

In a few more moments Major and Madame Ertmann stroll in,

trying not to look overawed, and followed by Countess
Erdody, who gives me a friendly nod. As they take their seats
Fritz has his violin in his hand and is already looking
nervously at his part. I take my seat beside him and smile and
he smiles back, a jigging, explosive smile. In his red tunic, hair
cropped, he passes well for a boy, not even a pretty one; our
audience will be used to seeing such raw youths make up the
numbers at the end of a season.

I know, as I look at him, that he knows I know, and fear that
he may be embarrassed: but he is not. I suppose he is used to
it: people who know he is a girl but put it to the back of their
minds, like Sophie and Linke, and who knows who else?
When our eyes meet I know that he is troubled by something
he cannot put into words. The pale eyes have a distant look. I
guess that it is not the performance that worries him: more
likely *he* senses change in the air. Linke's anxiety troubles
him. If he went to this farm I suppose he could, once more,
become a girl. If he went to Lichnowsky's, it seems that
Sophie would keep him disguised as a boy. I wonder which he
would prefer. My arm begins to rise as if to mime a melody –
La – La-La –La -: infinitely sad. Fritz giggles and looks away.

I hear a dull, irregular rapping of feet. Peter Andreyich has
come in and seated himself at the front, and Sophie has also
come in with two of the cooks, bearing trays of glasses, bottles
of champagne and buckets of ice. I wonder that Karl is not
present. When she has put her burden down Sophie looks
across and beckons me to her.

'You were looking at him!' she hisses.

'Of course,' I say, 'to help him. He's nervous.'

'You can leave that to Linke. I tell you: don't look at him.'

'I can hardly help it,' I smile.'Don't joke with me. I mean it.
The Count should have told Schuppanzigh to find someone
else.' I recall what Linke told me about the Count's finger and
Sophie, and decide on a little revenge. 'He's good enough,' I
say, 'and handsome!'

Sophie's glare is like sulphur, but before she can spring at me
the Count himself comes in with the Lichnowskys. The
Princess is on his arm, and his head is close to hers. He gives

Sophie a cold glance which makes her turn from us both and bury her head in her hands. They must have quarrelled again, but Sophie is perverse to suspect me with the boy.

Linke wanders in, his grey hair pulled into a knot. He has both quartet and cello sonata to undertake. Madame Ertmann will play piano. Behind him Schuppanzigh, bustling, cheerful, a little fearful of being late, enters with Beethoven and Madame Brentano.

Prince Lichnowsky wears his dull green. Rasumovsky wears his white. He has a clean, white bandage on his finger. Major Ertmann wears the black uniform of Austria, and his wife a black dress. Princess Lichnowsky is dressed in scarlet with jet beads at her throat. Countess Erdody wears russet with a necklace of little pearls. It looks as if their supper passed off without incident. Madame Brentano and Beethoven have favoured blue. Hers is a summer night's satin, made lustrous by a necklace of diamonds. His, worn for the first time, is almost black like a thundercloud. There is no Archduke Rudolph, after all.

We play as they sit in a half-circle around us and the grand piano, to one side the Ertmanns with Beethoven and Madame Brentano; to the other the little Countess, Peter Andreyich and the old Prince, with the Count and Princess in the middle. Sophie is standing near the door, watching them and us; her heavy shoe is visible. The Princess, leaning against the Count, suddenly looks at her and scowls, but the old Prince puts a mottled hand on her arm. Before I know it we are in the adagio and time momentarily stands still for all of us; then the trio, gallop, applause, and champagne for the guests.

Fritz has played well! Schuppanzigh kisses his roguish fingers to him. Linke smiles a brief, wry smile. I raise the boy's hand aloft, feeling the softness of his long and tapering fingers. The tray shakes in Sophie's hands.

'Really,' the Princess says to the Count, who calmly hands her a full glass, 'I am sure, Andrei, that the music is very good, but I am still concerned about the servants…' she indicates us and Sophie with a toss of her head. Beethoven looks at them, then walks over to us and begins to improvise at the piano. Prince

Lichnowsky looks up in alarm, but Antonie smiles at him and says: 'He doesn't mind us talking, sir.' The Prince bows his head and smiles at her. 'Such a g-g-genius you see. Every note is – such perfection. One hates to miss – well, anything. And yet,' he leans closer to her, dropping specks from his wig, 'I cannot help thinking that he has never bettered the *Eroica*.'

'My dear Andrei,' the Princess continues, putting her other hand in his, 'Prince Metternich says we must keep a firm hand, especially with our army away. Speaking of which, where is Karl? It seems we have nothing left but cripples!'

'I really don't know where he is,' replies the Count. 'It may be that the Prince only meant to lend him to us...''Even the musicians,' she says, turning to look at us and Beethoven. 'Look at that insipid child! And where is the blonde young man...'

'Mayseder? I do not know that either.'

Fritz puts away his violin and stands, putting the case on his chair, but he doesn't know where he should go. His lip trembles and I fear that the Princess will see what he is, but luckily she has turned away, pulling the Count across the room.

'The Allegretto pleased me,' she says, deciding to be more conciliatory. 'Dear me, that Russian folk-tune! It must make you think of this terrible new war we are in.'

'Of course,' says the Count, teasingly, 'Austria is Bonaparte's ally. You are fighting Russia.'

'Don't be absurd!' says the Princess. 'I mean, what if we are? Your Tsar will not give in. Russia will not give in.'

'Well, we might still agree a peace...'

'Never!' cries the Princess.

'I agree Princess!' Beethoven, suddenly hearing, shouts, as he prances by with Fritz, whom he has caught in a friendly head-lock: 'Russia won't suck his dick like us!' The Princess gasps and whirls about so violently that the Count has to catch and steady her. 'Oh Andrei,' she moans, 'why these dreadful people?' She has her arm about his neck. 'It's because you're not happy!' she howls. 'Remember when my sister was here: you, Elizabeth and I. Poor dead Elizabeth. That was better, was it not? Was that not true harmony?'

'God did not bless you with children, though.'

I do not know if anyone heard. It seemed to be a murmur that echoed: a woman's voice. Then, like a stung horse, the Princess rears back and rushes out through the door. The glasses on Sophie's tray glitter like shards of ice. Madame Ertmann goes to the piano in a taut, rippling silence. Only Countess Erdody claps and says: 'Ah, the cello sonata!'

Schuppanzigh sits beside the Major, who is as straight as he is round. Peter Andreyich sits down calmly beside Prince Lichnowsky, who says to him in a puzzled voice: 'I do have a son, you know: young lad in the army. Was a young lad, that is.' Peter Andreyich is looking at Linke and does not reply. The Count takes another glass from Sophie, but she looks at him with hatred. Still, I am sure it was not her. He turns calmly back to his seat, and Madame Ertmann and Linke begin.

Fritz and I stand quietly against the other wall. Sophie looks across at us. I watch Linke's elbow shake and drive, and I have a thought. I know a certain way to make Sophie banish the boy to Linke's farm: it is to make her more jealous. I take him about the waist and look into his puzzled eyes. I make sure Sophie is still in her place. Yes she is there, and looking. The rest are intent on the music. 'Look,' I say to Fritz, 'I'm going to kiss you now. Just a pretend one, don't be afraid.' He looks up, wondering, with the faintly derisive smile of a healthy, energetic young boy. I kiss him before he can squirm, quickly but long enough to hear the sound of breaking glass as a tray slips, once more, from Sophie's hands.

6. Mayseder

I have decided to join the Grande Armée and fight. France is invading Russia, and France is more enlightened, more equal, than any other country, even though Napoleon is allied to Austria. Maybe if he wins equality will spread. That is some kind of hope, and so it is better to go and fight than stay where I am. I take a coach north, up to Breslau, and then on towards Poland. I do not say goodbye to my parents: they could not understand. Thunderstorms sweep over the plains, and I am afraid. I have nothing but a small bag of clothes, a fiddle, and Rasumovsky's florins. If all else fails I can earn money from my fiddle. Everyone knows that the Grande Armée is moving towards the Russian frontier. Everyone knows that the kings of Europe were summoned to Napoleon at Dresden, before they dispersed to their spas. Austria fights alongside France, but she doesn't want to. Metternich stays in Vienna, keeping a watchful eye. So I have decided to join the French, and fight to free the Russian serfs. France has an Emperor, but still the French believe in liberty. People of all nations have joined with them to fight. My plan is to find a Polish company, for the Poles, more than any other people, still believe in liberty. While Rasumovsky sits in Vienna with Metternich, I will invade his country.

In these terrible last three years I have suffered paralysis. She has become all things to me, and I have been nothing to her: Therese! Your pale eyes follow me still, in my dreams, but no sun ever breaks through this shimmering haze. You and I stagnated in the swamp of the palace where I saw that your vile disguise had found its way into your soul, and that therefore, unless the palace could be cracked open like a rotten nut, you would always exist in a deathly dance of aristocrats. Besides, I always felt that she, and I because of her, was somehow being watched.

At first, when she did not (or could not) respond to the heart I offered, (even though she had grown from a child almost into a woman), after which of course I would have planned our escape, I went to the Schwan to drown my sorrows, or even to try and get some inspiration for my own music. I saw that fellow Karl, the Count's supposed servant, watching me, but we did not speak. Now and again Beethoven would call me across to his table. He would hum a tune of mine, and look at me sideways under his brows.

'Write some more, young puppy. Take it down to the Court Theatre. Show it to Salieri – mind he doesn't steal it though!' His eyes have lights like a brook in summer. A plague, he said, on tyrants near and far, who will not leave him be. Is our hope not in the common people I asked – Austrian, German, Hungarian? But he shook his head. In an unguarded moment I told him that I believe the people will one day prevail, and that therefore I intend to join the Grande Armée. When he heard me he roared like a lion, and then looked at me with sympathy and bewilderment. He turned to the paper beside him and jotted something down. He hummed. He did not show it me.

I am already in Warsaw, but I have seen no troops. My plan now is to find out one of Napoleon's marshals, to whom I can explain in French my desire to serve in the ranks. If I hold up a florin the inn-keeper brings me food, but no-one here speaks German I can understand, or any French, or gives me any change for my florins, and I have been here two days. No-one can tell me which coach to take next, or where the Armée is. The inn is not very clean. It's the kind of place where one might be robbed or murdered.

I am breakfasting next morning on some tough black bread when Karl appears. His presence makes me shudder, although in my heart it is not a surprise. Everyone in the palace knows that he is employed by Metternich. He sits down across the table, looks at me with his burning eyes, cracks a knuckle and asks me what I am doing here. Falteringly, I explain. It is not a crime, I suppose, to want to fight for Austria's ally. Besides I am of no importance. If he decides to let me go I might make my way back home. He ponders for a while, his face like a basilisk. Then he leans forward and tells me that, since I wish it, we will join the Armée together. In a whisper I ask him if he is not needed in Vienna, but I get no reply.

The next days are like a dream – a dream of naked terror and some excitement. Karl moves into my room. We dine together and if he takes a beer I take one too. At night I sleep fitfully, cowering inside. Then he takes my money and buys us horses. Two days later we have enlisted with some Polish cavalry, whose colonel speaks a little French. Armed with a sabre, my fiddle tied to my saddle-bow, I trot with Karl behind these Uhlans; and in a few days we join the line of march of the Grand Armée. I watch dogs and women on the roadside, flitting through the clouds of dust rising from half a million men, but fortunately we can ride across the fields. The Uhlans trot and swerve, and I struggle to keep up: but after a week my horse and I can jump a hedge, and I have a new moustache. Some Austrian troops, in their black, are marching and camping far to the right, on another road. Nobody here trusts them.

One night I am wrapped in a horse-cloth on the edge of the circle where we sit by our fire, lulled by the crackling of wood and the steady breathing of horses. Karl is stretched out on the ground. The Uhlans are passionate men. Their only real cause is freedom for Poland, although, I suppose, they have no objection to freedom for all mankind.

Suddenly a tiny creature swoops across my head and circles over the fire, cutting the smoke with its pointed wings. The Uhlans scream and it seems to answer. They are crossing themselves and rolling their eyes. One, a limber, fair-haired man with a serious expression, grabs a branch from the fire and waves the glowing end in the air. His boots send up a shower of sparks. The others jabber restlessly. Now the bat flits out of sight, up towards the dim stars, which seem to hide themselves above the trees. The Uhlans cannot settle down again, but keep on muttering, looking skywards and crossing themselves. My foot touches the fiddle with which I sleep every night, keeping it under my arm or in the crook of my leg, and I think, why not? I draw it up, undo the latches, draw out the bow and test the strings. I play the allegretto from the

MARK PAFFARD

second Rasumovsky; which, ironically, is a Russian tune. The
Uhlans nod in their friendly way, pleased to be distracted, and
finding something familiar in its gay seriousness; but I feel
Karl's cold eyes boring into my back.

I jump up and leave him, taking my fiddle with me, and I have
just begun to piss against a holly bush when I hear a splashing
which is not my own. I look through the leaves at a lean, dark
face, and a pair of bold, dark eyes. How handsome is his
moustache; how curled and pointed -and, indeed, how
familiar!

'En garde!' says Captain Ramballe, in jest. He does not
recognise me. I feel for the hilt of my sabre. Here, in front of
me, is the man whose callousness froze the springs of love in
Therese. 'Draw your sword!' I tell him. 'I am here to avenge
the honour of Therese Linke!' I feel as if my words are
perfectly natural. Indeed, they are the words I have spoken
many times in my dreams. Ramballe looks in astonishment.
Then I see recognition begin to dawn in his face. 'Ah, the
musician!' he says. 'What can you be doing here? And how
was the Count, when you last saw him? But I assure you,
Monsieur, that the young lady is safe, and not dishonoured.'

At this impudent denial, for I know exactly what he did to
Therese, I draw my sabre out in a fury, but when I raise it my
arm trembles at its weight. Then my wrist is caught by a strong
hand. Karl's other arm is on my left shoulder, his hand in front
of me is pointing a pistol at Ramballe. 'Come,' he says to me,
'better stick to your fiddle. You have no business whatsoever
with this man.'

'Ah!' exclaims Ramballe, appearing not to notice the pistol,
'the servant is here too! This is more than I understand.
Gentlemen, no doubt I will see you in Russia!' He turns on his
heel and walks back through the trees to his company. I return
to mine and lie down again, and quite soon I am overcome by
sleep.

Next morning the army moves on and we go with it, through
thunderstorms and mud. At last we emerge from the forest.
We learn that we are on the banks of the Niemen, and can see
the steppes of Russia. Now we are crossing on bridges. My

78

horse rocks on the shaky planks, and I have to cling to his mane. Looking back the way we have come we see the army stretched in the sun right up to the flat horizon.

As we cross the trampled grass I see Karl with our colonel, who is clearly impressed by his size and strength. The colonel is nodding and pointing, puffing his red cheeks in excitement while Karl sits motionless on his horse, looking towards a group of horsemen. As caps fly in the air around them and shouts go up, I see it is the Emperor. Hc is a small man on a white horse, wearing a grey overcoat, just like all the drawings and, as I had long expected, the whole army suddenly seems to bristle in his presence.

This night we have to lie down on the muddy plain. Karl's long arm encloses me, making it hard to breathe; but there are soft stars far and wide, all about the open sky.

At dawn we saddle and start to walk our horses forwards among the sprawling mass of troops, of whom many are still lying on the ground. The breath of thousands of horses and soldiers rises up like a fog. After a while we see before us the waves of a new river, seeming to bare its sinews in the pale light from the clouds. Karl has been with our Colonel again. When he returns he looks almost cheerful. He points to where the Colonel, more red-faced than ever, holds his horse and speaks to a huge, moustachioed officer, whose uniform is as fresh as if it were newly painted. It is one of the Emperor's suite – not far behind him the little, grey-coated ruler is busy with a telescope. The officer goes over to Napoleon, and then returns. The Colonel salutes and turns back towards us, beaming all over his face, and in a moment our whole troop breaks forward into a gallop. As my horse bounds under me I fear that I shall fly from my stirrups into the air, but soon we slow up behind the colonel, who has reached the river and, waving his sword in the air, forces his horse to leap from the shelving bank.

Everywhere horses' manes are floating in the stream, or sinking with their riders, until only the tips of upright lances are visible. Now Karl and I are in the river too. Suddenly a strong arm wrenches me from my saddle. I see fishes darting through clouds of mud, and horses rolling under the waves. I feel a vice-likc grip on my arm, and then I see no more.

***

When I wake I am lying in a covered cart, which is standing still among some trees. A moon is rising, faint, through the hangings, while through the cloth at my head the sunlight filters over my face, and by this I know it is evening and that the cart is pointed west, away from Russia. Looking down from my chest to my feet I see that I am dressed in peasant clothes. I try to move an arm and feel that I am very weak. I manage to turn on the straw and hear, right below my head, the noise of two people making violent love. When they have finished the woman tells the man he should stay with her, but he, Karl, says no, he stays with the young man.

'Is he worth keeping?' she asks, in a thick German accent, 'We will pass a monastery. Leave him there.' Karl pauses and then answers: 'Well - you never know.'

As the moon rises higher the cart begins to move. I try sitting up, in case I should need to escape, but I am still very weak, and I think my fever returns, for I remember nothing else, until Karl is carrying me on his shoulder across a field. I catch a glimpse of an old man and his dog. They bring me to some kind of tower and then they lay me down on another pile of straw. Karl, as he has done before, pours water between my lips. I am left alone. The light is dim, but not dark, and I can tell that outside the sun is shining brightly. It lights up a wooden staircase to the upper floor. The door to my left opens, and another path of light stretches in towards my feet. I see a plate at the end of a slim arm; on it a slice of black bread, some cheese and an apple. I close my eyes; but as the plate is put down beside me I feel a very gentle presence, and I cannot help looking up. A pair of eyes, very wide, more grey than blue in this light; a slim girl in peasant dress; a slender nose and a mouth closed hard in concentration, as though its owner was playing a difficult piece of music. Then the eyes blink quickly and I recognise Therese, who turns and very softly walks away.

In the evening Karl returns on one of the cavalry horses. He too is dressed like a peasant. He says he dragged me out of the river after we had been swept downstream and came out on the Polish bank. He has nursed me and brought me here, to recover my strength. It is just a small farm. We can sleep here, in the tower; he has arranged it with the old man. It will be best for us to stay here until the war has truly begun.

'Has it not begun?' I ask.

He frowns, and says there are rumours of peace. My mind is full of Therese, if she looked taller, and whether it was her at all, or another fever-dream, but Karl reads my thoughts and remarks that the girl whom Rasumovsky kept hidden in his palace is also here. He gives me a sly look that is almost friendly.

'You knew about her then?' I ask.

'Of course,' he says, 'I and the old man knew.'

'What happened to *your* woman?' I ask. He stares at me with coal-black eyes. 'When I was in the cart,' I say. 'Oh, the Jewess. I cut her throat.' He smiles reminiscently. I think he is making a joke.

The old couple almost remind me of my parents: that is, they are well-to-do, fearful and suspicious. They are in awe of Karl. But, of course, they are peasants: the old man wipes his nose on his sleeve.

I am set to hoe the rows of beans, potatoes, beetroot, and parsnip, which they use to make wine. I see Therese coming and going: she works indoors, or feeds the pig, or milks the cow. But the farm's wealth is in hops, which are grown for King Jerome, a lover of English beer. The building in which we sleep, with its oven and upper floor, is the drying-house. There are no farmsteads nearby, except for one ruin among the silent fields and woods surrounding the old man's land, which appears to be only the meadow around the buildings (farmhouse, tower and tottering stables), and the big field sloping gently upwards beyond it, in which the laden hop-frames stand like colonnades.

Therese and I have not yet learned to speak to one another, even when Karl is not on hand. He has suddenly gone to Prague, on business of his own. Most often it is now the old woman who waits on me. Sometimes she brings a broom and sweeps, or bends down and thumps the bed of straw. She has rather greenish eyes, in the shadow, and now and then smiles, gap-toothed, as if she did not dislike me. When Therese comes in her stead, I feel that I am in the presence of an angel. Once her disguise kept her from me, but now it is her beauty that makes her seem unreal; only now I am content just to be near her. If I had my fiddle, which must have been lost in the river, I wonder if I would dare, once again, to play her something: but I do not have it, and I have seen no sign that she has hers.

When Karl returns the old man takes him at once to look at the hops, which are ready for harvest. Karl leans towards him like a firm rock that leans away from its base: just as I remember him leaning, for a sign of attention, towards the Polish colonel; and as he once leaned towards the wizened figure of Peter Andreyich. I am told that I must learn to walk on stilts to cut free the hops from the frames, but the old man needs more labour for the harvest: the hops must all be cut and picked and then be stored and dried, but there are no neighbours to help. In the old days, he complains, blinking his pale blue eyes, which are oval like Therese's, it was easy to get some help since he could pay in silver coins; but now there are no neighbours, and besides no-one knows what these coins are worth. He looks at us suspiciously and tugs his patchy beard. His mouth is constantly pursed under a nose that seems too small for his gaunt and wrinkled face. Once, he goes on, he had two daughters and a son-in-law too, but none of them were any use; he was a fool to take in the grandchild. Promising him to solve the problem, Karl mounts his horse again and rides off across the fields. The old man relieves his feelings by glaring at me, before he stumps away to his parsnip wine.

This evening, after a day of clearing thorns and nettles from the garden, I mount upon my stilts from the base of the drying-house, whose bricks gleam in the setting sun. By comparison the farmhouse across the meadow is tumbled down and forlorn, its sagging roof ignored by the swallows that cluster above me here. The footholds on the stilts are impossibly high, but after several attempts I begin to balance my weight, and take a few steps close to the wall; but then, from this perilous height, the terrible smother of men and horses in the river flashes through my head once more and, for a moment, I am sure that I am going to fall. I grasp the tops of my stilts and force myself forward, forward. Suddenly I have some control. I follow the wall to its corner, and look round – and there, on another pair of stilts, with one hand on the wall, is Therese. We are face to face. And suddenly I can walk, though not, at first, very far. I step clear away from the wall, make a few steps over the grass, then carefully turn and hurry back to the wall. Therese watches me, and then she does the same, and I watch her. Soon we are both walking free. She catches me up with a wild smile. We step like giants around the farm, grinning down at the dogs that have come out to look at us. We step across the meadow towards the hops, whose tall rows loom towards us in the pearly light. As we pause on the gentle slope to look down the alley between them we see a canvas-covered cart resting among the apple-trees beyond. Behind it a thin smoke rises. Therese's elbow brushes mine, and then we hear, behind the hops, the old man's querulous, outraged, swearing. These Romani are filth he says: liars, unbelievers, thieves, and they bring the plague. When Karl speaks in reply we, both at once, drop to the ground and take our stilts home through the gloom; turning, as we cross the meadow, to look back at one another.

Karl, of course, has won his point: the Romanis will help us harvest these few hops in a day; and so, as soon as the sun has risen, we begin. Now Therese is truly an angel, floating on her stilts with me above the farm, stepping lightly in her long dress, while the wondrous light casts golden rays around her head. Up here with her I am invulnerable, even though I know that one should keep away from gypsies, who can not only pollute one's body with their frightful diseases, but also have ways of darkening a person's mind. But the Romani man is pitifully thin, though evidently strong enough. He wears one small gold earring and I see his teeth gleam white as he takes his orders from Karl. His woman, as hollow-eyed as he, is shapeless, ragged and dirty. There are streaks of mud on her breasts, which hang loose inside her gown. Lastly there are two children in rough petticoats, who hide beneath mops of hair, and flit across the ground like imps.

We stay aloft for two or three hours, loosening the bines to be pulled down onto the barrows and stripped. Therese's grandparents work together, keeping by themselves. There is a pink spot of bald skin in the old woman's hair. Karl works alongside the gypsies, setting the pace with his soldier's movements and constantly watching the children, who dare not disobey. The sun begins to beat on our heads so that, in spite of the light work and the gentle breeze, we are covered in sweat. At last Karl calls a halt, and we come down to rest and eat in what little shade remains. Over half the bines are cut, and now it will be left to me to bring down all the rest as the hop-picking goes on. Therese sits near the old couple. All three are smiling at the progress of the work. I look at her as she sits in the dirt, her golden hair in a tangle, and her damp breasts pushing out her smock. When she sees me looking she smiles, and, while no-one else is looking, raises her arms before her to imitate a fiddle.

I work through the rest of the cutting, and the labour of picking that follows. My back and arms ache ceaselessly, but I am happy, and suddenly it is late afternoon, the bines lie stripped, and the work is done. The gypsy harnesses his own horse to the second cart, and we all move off together, but Karl and the old man do not allow him into the drying house, pushing him back to pass the sacks to me, in the doorway, and then inside to the elders, who shuffle them over to Karl, who hoists them one by one and carries them up the stairs to the drying-room.

Jupiter rises beyond a crescent moon in the South. That must be the direction of Vienna. I help Karl to empty the first ten sacks of hops and spread them evenly across the drying floor. The old man lights the stove. Therese and her grandmother arrive smiling with chicken, bread and cheese, and large, clean potatoes to roast. Then Karl bends down in the straw and uncovers five bottles of wine. The label on them says

'Bordeaux', and he says he got them from a Frenchman he met in Prague. He opens the first with a corkscrew that he pulls from his pocket, and he gives us to drink. 'It tastes like currants,' says the old woman, 'and smells like chocolate.'

The old man feeds the stove from a basket of coal. Karl goes upstairs at intervals to check the hops, lifting his rake from its place at the foot of the stairs. We eat the good food and sit in the glow, watching the darkness thicken through the narrow windows, and passing round the wine. At last the old man begins to sing a slow, mournful song about Frederick of Prussia, and his wife joins in. Then, after telling Karl severely to mind the fire till morning, he takes her by the arm and they stumble out into the meadow, still surrounded by the sweet and sleepy smell of hops.

Karl sits like a shadow, looking towards the stove. I edge away into my straw-filled corner, and find that Therese is there. I give her to drink and she smiles and lifts her mouth to mine. Karl goes up the stairs. I hear him, faintly, raking the hops, as we gaze at each other and enter into paradise.

After our embraces and kisses and a delight too great to comprehend as yet, I fall asleep. Later I feel her slip away, and her lips on my forehead, but I am somehow unable to move. There is no need. But when I hear the stirring of birds, and Karl's footstep on the stairs, it is at once as if what happened was an illusion, one false gleam in the darkness of my mind. I huddle myself upright and fumble for my shirt. Like my fate he comes towards me: dark, impassive, filled with power. Like some magus he bends down and lifts up a single straw. It is red with blood.

As I get dressed he goes and stands in the doorway, looking out. There's a little blood on my groin. Suddenly I dash outside, ducking underneath his arm, knowing well that he will follow, wanting and not wanting him to speak. But he turns back inside, comes out with his saddle, fetches his mare who comes out snorting a quiet greeting, saddles her, and then at last comes across to where I have thrown myself on the grass.

'I must get away,' I tell him.

He nods, with a paternal air, understanding that it is all too much for me, too sudden. I must escape – escape and think – and find my work, my music again. I realise that I have always been afraid of her.

He tells me to wait where I am and canters over the meadow, past the dead bines and out of sight. As I lie on the grass in the dim light, with the first hint of the sun stretching out like fingers towards me, I hear wild barking, pistol shots and distant screams, which rise up for a moment like the climax of an aria. Karl returns, galloping, and as I stand up he seizes me by the shoulders and lifts me up in front of him. From the direction he has come a pall of black smoke is rising, just as the sky above it turns to cornflower blue.

We ride for more than a day and night, resting the horse every few hours and snatching our food from inns. As the landscape begins to seem more familiar I am impelled to speak. I hope, I say, that he is looking forward to Vienna after our strange adventures. Karl looks into the distance and spits.

'Mostly,' he says, 'I have wasted my time. I thought there was more to you than there is. However I am sure that the French and Russians will fight.' He fixes me with a cold look. 'You,' he says, 'will return, of course, to Count Rasumovsky. He will pretend not to care where you and I have been. That is his Russian cunning. Write more music for Princess Lichnowsky. Forget about that girl for now: she is Rasumovsky's toy, but remember everything you see in the palace. Remember that you are Austrian. It may be that Prince Metternich will ask you what you know. And remember that I will be watching you.'

I see that we are among the vineyards not far from the village of Heiligenstadt. I might meet my father out here. Soon the Danube will appear and, behind it, the spire of St Stephen's. 'Why did you kill them?' I ask.

'One picks off lice when one sees them,' he says, untethering his horse.

7. Linke

Three years have passed for my niece: more quickly, perhaps, for her than for me; now at last she is back in my apartment, where Anna and Sophie, working together, are dressing her. They are fitting her in black. The narrow gown holds her slender breasts while Sophie fiddles with a black wig to cover the unruly mop on her head as she is transmuted from pageboy back into girl. The wigmaker came to the palace, and no expense was spared to ensure a perfect fit. Soon Therese will go to the farm. I am not entirely sure why Sophie changed her mind, although I think it began while I was playing the cello sonata. Then when she suddenly dropped those glasses and the Count, in front of everyone, showed her such a tenderness (of course it brought back an incident that some of us recalled); and then Beethoven, Madame Brentano, Maria Erdody and the old Prince were so full of smiles, that it seemed that nothing might be impossible.But at this moment Therese is being dressed to perform. We are to give the first performance of an extraordinary new quartet, Opus 95, which Zmeskall has had for two years but has never had played. Stranger still, it will be performed while Beethoven is away. Most of Vienna is away. Somehow, between Schuppanzigh and the Count (though he, too, will not be there), it has been decided that for this one performance Therese will play first violin, while the great Schuppanzigh plays second. So Anna kneels in front of Therese, her mouth full of silver pins, and light sits on the panelled walls like the points of bayonets.

Sophie and I have come from the palace together, two of us with a limp, attracting the idle gaze of peasants unloading their grain. People starve elsewhere, but grain is cheap in Vienna, with so few to buy. I have heard the brothel-keepers use it to make a vile gin, hoping that somehow some soldiers will return: but, French or Austrian, they won't be returning soon, not now the cloud of war has rolled on, towards the Russians.

Here in Vienna it is hard to breathe: the air promises thunderstorms, but they never come.

I caught Sophie's foot, her swollen one, the other day. As she unlocked that odd little store-room where the pipe comes up from the kitchens I followed her in and caught it, as she clambered like a monkey up the ladder fixed to the wall. There is a trap-door in the ceiling that nobody would notice unless they were looking hard. I was looking for answers. She looked down and grinned, green-eyed.

'You win,' she said, 'she goes to the farm, I don't want her under my feet, but there's a price: there always is, for the likes of you and me. The Count has his plans for you. Oh, and while I'm away, make sure the little trollop doesn't entangle my husband.'

I have noticed, of course, that Weiss loves to play with Therese, but that's entirely innocent, and I believe that in her heart even Sophie knows it too. I wonder whether, after all, Therese might not stay here. Our neighbours have surely forgotten seeing her with the French Captain; in any case they have forgotten how they hated the French. But the decision that she shall play the new quartet, and in front of gossips like Zmeskall, will thrust her back in the limelight, and I dare not object. The Count's gold will sweeten the old man at the farm, and then Therese will be hidden away until we all know where we are.

In the Count's absence Anna and I will be of service to Countess Erdody, who is staying on in Vienna. We are to play in her salon. This spring she took me to Pest, where I performed in *King Stephen*; and then to her estate, where the husband was shooting, and did not get in the way. She and I have played together all of the cello sonatas, and she has learned to add to her playing some quick, elusive sparks of passion that she always had inside. *King Stephen* was to mark our Emperor's birthday; but now in Hungary there are rumours of trouble from hotheads, those Magyar moustaches, who might rise up while our army is in Russia. Maria Erdody herself is proudly Hungarian and longs for independence, but she hopes to further her cause here, through diplomacy.

'Sit down, Linke.'Rasumovsky sits down beside me on the chaise longue in his study. I remember how Sophie lay here: I can hear the birds and see the leaves on the poplar outside. Rasumovsky leans back, sighs.'Life is hard my old friend, no?'

'Sire,' I say, 'it is what it is.'

'Well,' he says brusquely, 'we must still try. It is not easy to keep everybody satisfied, neither in music, nor in life. That is why I require something more of you.'

I wait for him to get to the point – what I must do for him, in return for what he will do for Therese. I see that the leaves by the window are covered with a film of dust. I smell his eau de toilette and feel, by my side, the constant strength of his long limbs, the reach and iron claws of a bear.

He gives me my instructions. First, I am to escort Therese to the farm. From there I will travel on to a house in Prague, and stay one night. Officially I go there to make music for a friend of the Count's. From there I am to return to Vienna and Countess Erdody. When I am in Prague I will send a message by post to him at Gratz. He gives me the message I must carry and two bags of gold – one for Therese's board and one for my own expenses – and has me repeat everything he has said.

'You will be watched, of course,' he says when I have finished. 'All my servants are watched, as are Countess Erdody's, but you will not be harmed or questioned. Your message is not dangerous – it merely hints that this war might end in peace, and peace is in every country's interest. France might go back to fighting with England, or even make peace with them as well. If France and Russia weaken each other Austria might benefit, but that is not certain. If France and Russia come to an understanding, Austria knows she must be there. If Austria thinks that a peace is possible, it makes peace more likely. So it is worth a try. And you must convey my good wishes to Beethoven. You will see him there.'

Mistress Therese Linke is dressed, and her bow leaps like a flame, as she plays next to Schuppanzigh in our rehearsal at the little Countess's salon. Weiss and I stumble after them, causing Beethoven to chuckle. Sure enough, he is about to leave for Prague, while Sophie, who is here too, is going to Gratz with the Count. The crimson apartment, without a fire, is full of long purple shadow. The music, in the afternoon's peace, leaves us in calm astonishment, as Beethoven absently kneads Sophie's neck and shoulders. Countess Erdody herself has gone to the Rasumovsky palace. We are left alone.

'Are you happy?' asks Beethoven. 'Does he beat you, your Count?' Sophie looks across at Weiss, who is looking into space.

'It is not always easy,' she says. 'But, sometimes, I am happy, yes.'

***

Now Rasumovsky, Sophie, and Beethoven have all gone their ways. The night of the performance comes. We have packed up all our things, for the Count's second coach is waiting to take us all away at midnight. In the Countess's bright and now overheated salon, Prince Metternich is sitting next to a Russian lady, who is evidently bored. She has the round red cheeks of a Russian doll with small, sharp features to match, and an enormous bust. The Chancellor of Austria leans his flaxen hair towards her raven tresses, and feasts his eyes upon those breasts of startling white. In the warm air the candles bow in tribute to his elegance. Schuppanzigh says softly to me: 'I shall miss you this summer, Lefty. I hope things work out for you.' I look at him in surprise, but I can see at once that he is not part of any secret plan. I try to put the impending journey out of my mind. 'As long as we get through tonight,' I say. 'Oh the quartet will be all right. We have practised have we not? It is his love-song – we must play!'

'It is Opus Ninety-five!' Weiss steps in excitedly. 'Have you noticed? Fifty-nine backwards! Does The Master mean something by that? 'Probably not,' says Schuppanzigh. Weiss nods in his rabbit way, but looks quite unabashed. I have rehearsed but not grasped it yet; I have not lost the habit of being anxious for Therese, even though Schuppanzigh, happily playing second, revels in their partnership. It is a pure, strange music, but whether it speaks of love, or what kind, I am quite unsure.

Countess Erdody has a kind nod for stony-faced, stooping Peter Andreyich, who is taking his meals with her, and a kind word each for Nikolaus Zmeskall of the Royal Hungarian Chancellery, Gentz the Imperial Secretary, Carl Beethoven of the Treasury, and even for the gallows-high, bony, secret, Salomon Rothschild, banker and incarnate Jew. She comes to Prince Metternich and, very respectfully, embraces his new mistress, Princess Bagration, wife of the Russian general. Then she asks straight out what news there is of the war.

'In war, as in love, Countess, nothing is certain until the end.'

'But do you think,' says the Countess, in French, 'there is any chance of peace?'

'Perhaps,' says Metternich coldly, 'you should ask Count Rasumovsky. I can only tell you that our troops are in the field.'

'I know that man Rasumovsky,' says Princess Bagration. 'Very clever man, they say. But his father was a peasant. Just like my husband. Just like Bonaparte, you see?' Metternich glances away, at Rasumovsky's uncle. Peter Andreyich gazes before him, in a world of his own, or maybe not familiar with the French of which even I, these days, can usually get the gist. He somehow effaces himself in the Countess's salon, blending with the honoured officials, in spite of the flavour of dust that clings to him no matter how often he has been brushed. Anna holds a tray of glasses. As we all drink champagne, the Countess plays and sings *Adelaide*, and we are charmed. Salomon Rothschild leans down to me and says: 'You musicians, Herr Linke, have a great future before you whoever wins the war. Music will be much in demand. I shall be at your service if you wish to invest your earnings.'

The thought of success, of real security, makes me feel strangely elated. To have a little house like Schuppanzigh, independence and money in the bank. Yet I don't see how a mere cellist could achieve it, especially when Austrian money is worth almost nothing.

The Countess makes her signal and we sit down to play. Prince Metternich, to judge by his face, finds it odd to have found himself among a band of paid musicians, who are not in livery; but his surprise is more than doubled when Therese appears. Whether the fact that she plays first and Schuppanzigh second is noticed by him I doubt, but I know that as we surge into the allegro, he is pinned like an insect by shock and indignation. I am grateful now that Therese is well disguised. A love-song, Schuppanzigh says, and he may be right, but also a rebel's dance. I close my eyes and see Beethoven, (clothes crumpled, hair in knots) dancing and roaring with laughter. It is full of his quirks, and yet it seems to stand apart. Last week Maria took me to Baden, dressed as her servant, to see a play of Shakespeare named 'As You Like It', which I did not understand. It was a story of lovers and clowns, and as full of quirks as this.

The officials, Zmeskall especially, ogle at Therese, but I can see that most of them are slowly captivated. Metternich sends another glance towards Peter Andreyich, but he, more than ever, is unflinching in his attention, watching our fingers with his hard, watery eyes. When it is over no-one speaks. Only Princess Bagration heaves a bosom-shaking sigh. Metternich asks, with an effort, whether Count Rasumovsky has also heard this piece? No, indeed, replies the Countess; for this is the first performance tonight, in honour of its dedicatee, this gentleman here, Herr von Zmeskall. Zmeskall gets a sour look. As he departs Salomon Rothschild gives me a bony, roguish smile.

***

Therese has taken off her wig and changed into her new, clean, peasant clothes: the hard-wearing smock and skirt. Her fair hair is somewhat grown but still rough, like that of a prisoner prepared for the guillotine. Anna and Maria wave our coach farewell. We rumble through the silent streets and across the Danube into the eastern plain. Disregarding Schuppanzigh's grunts I undo the window. It is warm, dry and clear. As the horses beat through the dust I bend my neck to look right up at the pure and distant stars in the shifting, inky sky.

At Olmutz my niece and I get down. It is early morning. Weiss and Schuppanzigh grin and wave, as Rasumovsky's carriage takes them onward to Gratz. In the lumbering wagon that we take to Breslau we are ignored by the one or two merchants, who only look askance at the cello. By mid-day we are alone. Therese unlocks her violin, and plays. We play together. The carriage bumps and jolts, and squeals our strings. There is cacophony, wind and rain, the forests and the rumbling wheels. My niece's eyes are very blue, and I think I will never love her quite so much as now. I have been used to seeing her every day in the palace. She will probably miss it too: life will be dull on the farm, but at least she will be hidden from prying eyes until we can decide what next; and she is still young, so young.

'I'm glad you played with us,' I say, to console us both.

'I am grateful, uncle.' She looks down wearily; her feet, for once, dead still in their clogs. 'You all helped me,' she adds: 'you, Schuppanzigh and Herr Weiss too.'

'Yes,' I smile, 'we even made a love-song for Prince Metternich!' Therese shakes her head at this. 'I think,' she says, 'this music is lonelier than that.'

When we reach the farm she smiles rather wanly, and then hands her fiddle over to me.

**

The coaching-inn on the Oder's island smells of new wood and varnish, and is spotlessly clean. Even the straw in the yard is clean. It is cleaner, I think, than the Rasumovsky palace, into which the dust of Vienna endlessly seeps. I look across the river towards the little spires of Breslau, thinking of the cannon that blasted the town from this spot. Up there Anna and I visited Weiss and Sophie in the little house by the ruined church. But when I came back to fetch Anna she had returned to Vienna, needing to finish an important customer's dress. I have no desire to visit the town again. It was never my home and nor is anywhere else. War, I think, moves like a series of open sores, from here, to Vienna, to Russia. As I travel on next day in the carriage to Prague, I see scattered fields of rye dotted across the plain like great golden tablecloths; but the peasants I see from here to Prague are like starved, bewildered dogs. Their lords, who never helped them much, no longer help them at all.

'Ho, Lefty, have you hobbled all the way from Vienna?' Beethoven stands before me in swallowtail coat; his chin smooth, his hair well-brushed and perfumed, his fingers calloused but clean right down to the nails. His face is half merry and half fraught with racing clouds. When Madame Brentano is announced his expression changes to one of glorious sun.

We are in a splendid house on the edge of Prague. Outside a grey, smooth twilight; inside candles lit, and a large fire of logs which overheats the room. Sitting beside it is my new employer, Count Rasumovsky's acquaintance, and I, for the occasion, am leader of his musicians, who are a motley crew. This new Count, so far as I can see, is from the box of petty Counts – one can tip them out like chessmen – grey-haired, paunched and jowled, long-nosed and arrogant. His housekeeper sits close by, filling his cup and plate. There is a whiff of Sophie about her – a greenish flash of the eye, and a half-pretty, half-wolfish smile.

In the stuffy drawing-room we play Hummel, Haydn, Cherubini, Salieri, Mozart– on and on and on. It is like struggling through a dark forest with hardly a flash of light or life. This Count Panderewski's specialty is original scores, which are brought in from the library and tumbled out before us. We play some of them from sight. No doubt he has his eye on a score from Beethoven, but at present he is simply in his cups. We play a tune by Joseph Mayseder. I wonder where he is.

And here, too, is Rasumovsky's erstwhile servant Karl. He has attached himself to another guest, the Comte de Périgord, better known as Bonaparte's ex-minister, Talleyrand, as well as, later, the Tsar's adviser. It occurs to me that he must have something to do with Rasumovsky's plan. I have heard of him from Ignaz, who met him once in Vienna, and said that he was like an ivory-handled razor. It is curious, then, to watch his cold eyes warm at the sight of Antonie Brentano, and see his Frenchman's heart bow down to her as she stands, radiant, in her velvet gown. Karl is a chained monkey beside him, looking bored and morose, and though it is obvious that he spies for Metternich, and that I am being watched, just as the Count predicted, I no longer fear for myself. He may be a dangerous fellow, but it's all too absurd.

Beethoven improvises at the piano, passing time as best he can in this strange company. He plays for himself and Antonie, caressing trills and sudden chords. He hunches up and the opening bars of the Opus 95 quartet explode into the stuffy room. Madame Brentano hears and smiles. Our flautist, a buxom maid, no doubt with a soldier husband, has already thrown her cap at me. As I stand by the door Madame Brentano approaches.

'I know, Herr Linke, you will not mind if I ask you, for myself only, how *was* the quartet, the Serioso?' 'Serioso' – of course, Opus 95. I tell her it was well received except, perhaps, by Prince Metternich. She tells me that she cares more for what the musicians thought, but she seems satisfied with the expression on my face. I think of Therese on the farm, and pray that one day she may blossom like this woman, who is indeed as grave and still and vibrant as a flower at night. For the life of me, I cannot picture Therese as either a wife or a kept mistress. Yet one of these she surely must become, or else a nun. I wish that Beethoven and his Antonie had been there, to hear her play. And would they have agreed with what she said – that it is lonely music?

Talleyrand appears from nowhere and looks me up and down. Karl watches like a hawk.

'You are one of Count Rasumovsky's musicians? You must give him my greetings. Say that I advise him towards friendship with Austria. This war will be very costly both to Russia and France.'

The players, hungry, shuffle away; the candles gutter out by themselves. Talleyrand takes his leave after a few more words with Karl. His carriage waits outside. Our host snores in his chair, leaving his guests, with the aid of the servants, to find their beds. The flautist is very willing, especially for a gentleman with one gold pièce to spare. She has noticed my hands. They do.

When she has gone to find her own bed I hear two muffled

steps on the landing outside: the tell-tale sign, I think, of a heavy man with a weapon, and knowing my door is unlocked (there is no key), I shiver at the thought that I am pursued by Karl. The first chirrups of sparrows embroider the morning mist. When I believe he is gone I slip from the bed and dress. If someone is watching me now I do not care. Here is Beethoven's room, and here is Madame Brentano's. Pretending to stretch and yawn I suddenly kneel down, look through her keyhole, and see their bedside candle, as if by magic, still alight. They are both sleeping like babies.

As instructed I take my morning walk into Prague, still reckless of my life. I post my message to Gratz. When I return to the house Beethoven and Antonie have departed, and neither is there any sign of Karl. Prague is a fine city of churches. I fetch away my cello and find the coaching-inn again and, a few hours later, I am on my way to Vienna, wondering if everything has been a kind of dream.

***

'He only attends to the cello,' says Maria Erdody. She has grown almost fond of Peter Andreyich, who looks at her with pleasure, as if she (or he) were a child. She is in friendly competition with Prince Metternich himself, who has the old man to dine with him and then sends him back, like a letter that has been unsealed and then sealed up again, returning more crumpled and inscrutable than ever. I myself am so used to his gaze that I find it less disturbing now; and when he dines, with scrupulous manners, an old man with his mind on his food, it is hard to credit his cold dislike of Sophie. We are in the habit now of playing him the cello sonatas, and he indulges us with his stillness, while that gaze, more piercing than ever, seems almost to lance my fingers. Maria is right: he never glances at her or at the piano. Sometimes he looks sad. Maria thinks he is anxious for Russia, and that he fears for the Count. 'For,' she says, 'Count Rasumovsky is no longer young, to be so unsettled. It is not good for a politician to be without a wife, an *establishment*.' I am surprised that Maria finds Sophie half at fault for the old man's dislike. She thinks that Sophie could hide her passions, be more the simple 'housekeeper'; but then she does not know about the Count's private late-night concerts. I have my own idea: that Peter Andreyich is disturbed, one might say made jealous, by Sophie and Beethoven. In our early days in Vienna Beethoven would go to their little cottage - I saw him once through the open door when I passed by - simply to gaze at her. The roughness that I love, especially in the cello, the unexpected phrase was, once, inspired by her, and I think the old man hates that she should somehow be a part of *his* beloved music.

A letter comes to Maria from Rasumovsky at Gratz. Rasumovsky reflects on the strange fact that most of Europe is at the spas, as if this were an ordinary summer, while his country suffers. Of the invasion he knows no more than us. It is common knowledge that the Austrian troops have reached Smolensk with the French. The town is devastated. The Grand Armée might withdraw until the Spring, leaving a chance for peace. 'I have heard from Prague,' he adds, 'that The Master makes terms with his Mistress. But that is between ourselves, who wish them well.' A strange expression, Maria remarks, in front of the servants. Is it, perhaps, some kind of code? *The Master...* who is that? I shudder at this game of words which I do not understand.

The Count himself returns at last with Sophie, before setting out for Karlsbad, Prague and Berlin. The news is out of a sudden – Moscow has fallen, and so he does not need me to tell him that Talleyrand was right.

I return to live at the palace. Maria and I have not tired of each other, but it is time for a pause. I am also conscious that we are always being watched. Karl has returned and resumes his duties as Peter Andreyich's valet, towering over the pale old man who still busies himself with dusting the statues. Therese is expected at Anna's; Rasumovsky himself will bring her on his return. He will also bring Schuppanzigh, Weiss and Hans, who have, it appears, also been employed on his errands; and I have also heard that Mayseder has suddenly reappeared at his parents' house, where no doubt he is being welcomed like the prodigal son. As we wait for more news from Moscow or St Petersburg, life here is taking on the semblance of a reunion.

So, as if nothing has happened (and has anything really happened?) I take back my room on the ground floor, and Natalie brings me my meals. The plump French maid asks nothing of me but a little pleasure. When I ask her what *she* dreams of she shrugs. Beyond the little games we play, she never tells me what she wants. All she will tell me of herself is that she came here from Paris many, many years ago. One day I tell her how I looked through the keyhole at Beethoven and Madame Brentano. She rolls her eyes, smiles cunningly, and then looks grave. 'Don't you think it was wrong?' I ask her. I want her to say so, and to forgive me for looking, when I had no reason but my awful curiosity. 'Why,' she says, 'I don't think they would care if they knew it.' She wraps me in her plump arms and kisses me again. 'Love makes them unafraid. I am glad to think of it.'

Sophie, now alone in the cottage, asks me to walk with her. She is going to the Stepansdom. No doubt she has something to tell me, away from the palace's prying ears, so I speak, in case we should be followed, in our Breslau dialect. Only when we have reached the cathedral do I understand that she is going to pray. Indeed, I had thought she was Lutheran, like Weiss, but I see her go to confession. I sit down and wait for her, looking up at the numerous flies crawling across the panes of stained glass.

'Show me Vienna,' she says, when she comes out: 'I hardly know it.' I show her the Augarten where the Thursday concerts are, the Burg and the Bastion, Streicher's music shop and the Karnthnerthor Theatre.

'So that is where the operas are,' she says, looking suspiciously at the low, ornate porch. I think of the times I have been in the orchestra there – Mozart, Gluck, Cherubini. 'So that is where those rich young women flaunt themselves,' says Sophie, 'that sort who give their bodies for a string of pearls.'

We wander back into the wide, bare parks, where the roses lag breathless on their stems, and sit down on a bench. Here we are in Vienna, neither poor nor rich, free to wander at will, but always afraid of others and ourselves. I remember how I once

told Schuppanzigh of a fine violist, steeped in his own
church's music and easily moved to tears, and how he and
Sophie and the boy made that first journey with me here,
where she became what she is. But, as with Maria, there is
comfort in being with another cripple, as if we really
understand each other better.

'I have not been in a Catholic church,' she says, 'since my
mother took me as a girl.' (I remember going to confession
with Father Gregor, all those years ago: I did not say all my
prayers. I took sinful pride in my playing.)

'You had much to confess then,' I say: 'where did you begin?'
'I could not tell the priest,' she says. 'I have not been good to
Hans. I left him alone because I was – busy. I was too proud as
well – he wrote that quartet for me, and now Hans doesn't care
for me, and the other one is dead!'

And what, I think, of the sins of the flesh? But those, I think,
could not be helped, and cannot now. She is thinking of three
years ago, when her baby died – she could not help that either
– almost exactly when Therese was turned into Fritz, and it
was Sophie then who took care of her. I owe her something for
that.

'Do you think,' she asks, 'that when I am dead my soul will
see her, my daughter? Is she in heaven, Josef?'

'I would think so,' I reply, 'since she never saw the world.'
There is another word: limbo. I am not sure that Sophie knows
it.

'But will I see her?' she asks, 'Even if I cannot repent?'
'Of course,' I say, 'of course.'

We hobble slowly back to the palace, each alone with our
thoughts, and yet in some kind of harmony. Soon the Count,
and Weiss, will return, the palace will be fully open, and
Sophie will resume her busy, passionate life. And I – what will
I do? She at least knows her future. I am quite uncertain.

I get up early, alone, next morning, among the chatter of birds
from the palace gardens; but there, in the corridor, outside the
old man's rooms, stands, like a raven, the brooding figure of
Karl. He looks at me as I pass him with eyes like a basilisk,
and as I set out for the market he does not bother to hide

himsclf; he lounges after me as if he were mocking my gait. I buy a thick pair of debrecener – smoked Hungarian pork and paprika; shallots; tomatoes; bread and fruit; a flagon of white country wine and a heap of little baklava. It is time for a holiday, and I will not let him spoil it.

Anna, barefoot, warm from bed, has just brushed her hair. It streams down between her shoulders as I turn the locks and bolts. Then I look down from the window. Of course he is standing there, but I am at home, secure. The fellow thinks himself dangerous but, like the boys I had to grow up and fight with, he is, in the end, a buffoon. If he had license to meddle with me he would have done it, right there in the palace, when no-one was around. We eat slowly and slowly we undress each other as the sunlight warms the room. Anna is beautiful this morning. We drink, talk, and eat baklava. We make love, lie down, and rest.

I sleep, and wake, and think again that this fellow is just playing games of his own. If his masters wished it I would be in jail, or worse. Metternich's people need no warrant. Would the Count protect me? No.

'Is he gone?' I ask Anna.

She is by the window, dressed, but her hair is still a long dark waterfall.

'Yes, he's gone. I should tell you, Josef, he spoke to me in the street the other day. Do you know what he said? He said he had seen my daughter at Breslau, and that she was well. That was strange, was it not?'

People say that the dead are well. That was in some other play Maria took me to. I look at Anna to see if she has read my thoughts, and I am reassured by her calm and satisfied look. In here we are cut off from the heat and stench outside, and a lingering spice and sweetness hovers in the air. If only Therese were here as well! I remind myself the fellow is a clown, and yet I know I will live in torment until she returns. Although I embrace her fondly, and keep my thoughts to myself, Anna is sad when I suddenly leave.

'What's your trouble?' Natalie asks.

'I don't know. Where's Madame Weiss?'

'Busy cleaning her cottage. She expects her husband soon. But what *is* your trouble?'

'Too many secrets,' I mutter. I am in the library, hoping that Sophie can give me news of the Count's return. Our music-stands are still in the corner, waiting for life in the palace to resume.

I already have Sophie's word that Therese will go back to Anna, not to the palace; she may play the fiddle discreetly, now and then. She will learn to sew and embroider, and be out of the reach of prying eyes, unless perhaps she should play among friends only, perhaps at Countess Erdody's. Natalie plumps up her breasts, as if she thinks this will distract me. 'As you told me a secret,' she says, 'I will show you another. But we must be careful. It would be terrible if anyone should see us.' Her eyes sparkle, and I know she means Karl, who treats her with cold disdain, and I can see that she in return craves a little danger and mischief, as if to make a fool of him. She closes the library door, and then leads me up the twisted staircase, up to the higher shelves of books, and, making sure we are unobserved, through a hidden door. There is a faint, stale odour which surprises me. The low-ceilinged room contains very little but a massive bed. Tapestries cover every wall, but the figures on them are half-hidden in shadow. I lift up the rug, and find the trapdoor to which I saw Sophie ascend. Natalie nudges me: it is time to go back. The windows are round like a ship's and the room seems to rock gently in the hazy light. I gaze towards the horizon, where the tall houses seem to sway to an unheard tune. Below and to my left is the cottage, where Sophie is beating a rug. The leaves sway in front of my face, and the birds dart back and forth. So this is Rasumovsky's lair: he too has need of one. Suddenly I understand that what will be, will be, and, at least for a precious moment, I feel utter peace.

8. Schuppanzigh

Weiss and I arrive at Gratz, the home of Prince and Princess Lichnowsky. The drive, festooned with weeds, rumbles and squelches beneath our wheels, the grass on either side is uncut, and the ironwork of the front door is covered in rust. How such ingrained dereliction would shock Mechthilt! I hope that my sweet, strong and good-natured wife will miss me just a little – as perhaps I will miss her. I know she will not pine. As for me, I've been here before, and in better days; but, for some reason I can't explain, I was never so excited.

The central pediment, like a Greek temple, still stands tall and white, but on both wings the roof leaks and cows eat the thatch in the stables. The servants are housed, higgledy-piggledy, on ground floor, in attic, or outhouse. On the upper floors, whose panelled grandeur hides the worst of the blight, there is plenty of room for our three aristocrats, the family Weiss, and myself.

From his office in a sound part of the East Wing, Count Rasumovsky looks down at the remains of the gravel drive. His body seems to be tensed like a wrestler's, as if to grapple with whole armies, or provinces, but I try not to remember his magnificent physique. He is much occupied with his correspondence, diplomatic or otherwise. He says, however, that he knows as little about the war as the Silesian peasants in these Silesian fields.

'Nor,' he adds, as if I too were a politician, 'am I sure what policy Russia should adopt. The odds look overwhelming. Yet if he wins what can Bonaparte do with Russia? Neither the Tsar nor the people will submit – my country will simply burn. And now we have Austria following France to war, when what it really wants to do is maintain its old, decrepit, mediaeval regime and to keep Hungary down; when we should all be working for peace and civilisation... ' It is raining again. He sniffs at the must in the room.

'You do not care for Prince Metternich,' I suggest.

'No such thing, and I shall make much of him when I return. He, perhaps, does not care for me, but peace would suit him very well. It might be the beginning of a civilised Europe. Austria's troops are already hanging back. If he thought that Bonaparte might be ready for peace, even now, he would propose it himself. The Hapsburgs should know it is hard enough to hold Spain and the Netherlands, without adventuring into Russia! I believe the Prince is at Karlsbad, or Teplitz. I must write to him, but the post these days…how, by the way, do you think he enjoyed this new quartet, of which you think so much?' He points at the score, which I have brought him from the Countess Erdody's.

'To Zmeskall!' he snorts. 'Well, Schuppanzigh?'I describe to him the soirée at the Countess's. He listens with close attention, making me feel obliged to omit no detail: the presence of Rothschild, Princess Bagration, the playing of Therese…'Is she so fine then?' he interrupts. 'Oh, quite unique: yet I would say that her natural gift is not, primarily, that of an ensemble player. She reminds me of Bridgetower…'

'And, you say, she could play this love-passion, as you call it, while Prince Metternich was dallying with the general's wife! It was hardly the kind of music to suit his type of amour. But you must get this dedication changed – I will pay for it. I deserve it. Or you can tell Beethoven to write me another such, when he is not too occupied with Madame Brentano. When I find out whether *he* is at Karlsbad or Teplitz, I will send you there.'

Young Hans Weiss is not unpopular with the other boys. Half-reluctantly, I think, he moves down from those rustling, leaking, musty garrets, from which one can sometimes hear the lovely laughter of simple young men, into his parents' rooms. They and I have a whole suite looking over the Prince's orchards, above and behind the Count, who has only to ring his bell for Sophie from below. The rooms are furnished with too many chairs and tables, all of which shake on their walnut lions' paws, along with a broken chaise, and a four-poster bed which no longer has its curtains. I see my face, fat and leering, in the ormolu codpiece of a high-backed rococo commode. Some of the window-panes are broken, bringing in the gentle flutter of insects in the warm summer nights, and the sharp sudden screech of an owl nearby; or else just the soughing wind and the steady, pattering rain.

I sit down with them, late, to share their bread, cheese and beer. Hans, with his red hair shimmering beside a candle, looks at me with eyes that sparkle and make me hold my breath. Sophie, of course, has made friends with the cook.

'Beer, these days, is p-p-patriotic!' she says. Everyone at Gratz drinks beer and everyone, almost from habit, imitates Lichnowsky's stutter. The Prince's depleted stocks of wine are reserved for his evening meal.

Franz Weiss glows contentedly. Or does he? Part of his always dreamy mind is always somewhere else. We all sit quietly, until I call for music. Then he blushes. I have no doubt that he remembers the quartet at Countess Erdody's, when his eyes seemed locked forever onto young Therese's face. Sophie remarks that we shall be overheard.

'Pianissimo!' I say.

'Come, darling, darling, blackbird, starling…' Weiss has his arm round her waist.

'Why not make music just for ourselves? You can hear the new quartet. Opus Ninety-Five!' He flourishes his score.

'Oh,' she frowns. 'And do I want to?'

'Yes-yes-yes-yes-yes!'

'Yes-yes, yes-yes' I join in, and then Hans, his face alight: 'Yes-yes, yes-yes, yes-yes, yes-yes, yes-yes-yes-yes, yes and yes!'

'The Allegretto!' I say.

'Yes,' says Weiss. 'Will you play first - this time?'

'Of course,' I say. 'Are you viola?'

'No, I'm second. I'll tune up higher. Here, Hans, where's your viola? You just follow the score. Don't worry.' Hans brings out his Guarneri, and I gape. It looks like honeycomb in his freckled hands.

'So,' laughs Sophie, 'am I the cello?'

'Well, you've heard Linke play. Just make some groans!'

We lay the score down on the floor and huddle above it – I on a chair and the three of them on the unsteady chaise beside me. How, I think, the Master would enjoy this massacre! For she groans well, trying to follow, and we all muddle our notes, and still the melody hums inside us. Hans grins and takes my breath away. I try to confine my gaze to his freckled hands.

Sophie is helping out in the kitchen, but Weiss and I, and the better half of his servants eat, in the country fashion, below the Prince's table. The *Eroica* was once rehearsed in this hall. Beethoven asked me to come then, but Lobkowitz had already hired me. The other daughters of Countess Thun, married respectively to Lobkowitz and to Rasumovsky, vied to have the best music, but it was Prince Lichnowsky whom Beethoven preferred, and our Princess Christiane Lichnowsky was the music-loving queen of Vienna then.

At the high table Count Rasumovsky mentions the new quartet. The Prince must see the copy of the score that he has received. Lichnowsky looks up, with sauce upon his chin. He has aged thoroughly now, whereas the Princess has no more than a wrinkle or two at her throat, and the Count one very small bare spot on his crown. The Princess states that she has heard from her friends in Vienna that von Beethoven has gone completely insane. His new work is tuneless and mad. His brother or his friends have sent him away, to be confined or cured.

'Well,' says her husband cautiously, 'we can make our judgement from the score that the Count has brought.'

'But you always adore him!' retorts the Princess. 'You both encourage him in his crazy ways. Although we had to bar him this house after he made a scene and insulted our army…'

Prince Lichnowsky looks down at his plate: 'Actually, my dear, they were French Officers…'

Everyone knows this old story. 1806. We were at peace, but the French had just smashed Prussia, and then captured Breslau. Beethoven refused to play for some officers and left this house on foot. 'And then he smashed Prince Karl's bust!' the Princess says to the room. 'Ah, the artistic temper!' says the Prince, 'but surely my dear, you remember that we forgave him? Indeed, last year, my dear, we all – he smiles vaguely down to us, the musicians - gave a performance of his *Mass in C* in this very room - and I, at least, found it sublime.' The Princess looks about her wildly. 'That,' she snaps, 'was God's work, not his!'

A few minutes later she asks, as she does each day, about the progress of the war. The Count replies, as he does each day, that, as far as he knows, the Tsar is standing firm. Perhaps, he adds today, Bonaparte will cease to advance. If the Russian army retreats it would extend his supply lines too far.

'Ha!' the Princess exclaims. 'And why should not *we*, and the King of Prussia, cut off his supply lines? Then he would be caught in a trap!' The Count smiles dryly. 'A better hope is that Bonaparte and Tsar Alexander call a truce. The French are having problems in Spain.' 'But surely,' the Princess retorts, 'the Tsar will want to give him the beating he deserves!' 'The Tsar will do what is right for Russia. He cannot match France, and if he could a strong Russia is not what Austria really wants. Bonaparte and the Tsar made one accord at Tilsit. They could always renew their vows.'

'Their *vows,* Andrei? What do you mean?' 'I was thinking of what, according to Prince Metternich, Bonaparte said in Paris, after the meeting at Tilsit (I, of course, was there): he joked that, if the Tsar was a woman, he would make him his mistress.' Sophie, who has just brought in some dishes for the sideboard, smiles openly across at the Count. 'Disgusting!' yells the Princess. One dish flies to the floor as she marches from the room.

The household dozes uneasily after lunch. I am thinking of fire. This morning, in the wormy chapel, where Weiss and Hans in the gallery accompanied a squawking *Credo*, we prayed for the nuns of Baden whose convent, with much of the town, has been burned to the ground. Now I imagine the sisters huddled together, raising their hands in prayer as the fire licks at their habits, rises up to their waists and sets crowns of flame on their snoods; until they all collapse in a heap of ashes. Fire could easily break out here, especially now the sun has dried out every pile of straw and lath of rotten wood. The servants go about with candles in their pockets. The cooks are not to be trusted. I remember the smoking ruins when Vienna was shelled, and then the news of that terrible fire in Paris. Many nights I have woken up thinking that I can smell smoke.

To ease my unrest I stroll through the box-tree maze. The air is hot, humming with flies, and heavy with the smells of honeysuckle, wild garlic and the newly-cut grass which has been raked to one side. Strolling on I hear the sultry notes of a clarinet. It sounds out again and then stops, and I follow to come upon Hans sitting on the ground, cross-legged like a flame-haired Pan. His shirt is halfway open, showing some freckles across his breast. His legs are taut and slender in his threadbare breeches, and his tunic lies beside him on the ground.

'No, no. Don't get up.' I lower my bulk carefully, as elegantly as I can, until I am down beside him, into his scent of musk and cherries. He has stopped playing, of course, and as I come to rest he smiles a quick, disarming smile: a smile, dare I think, of affection?

As casually as I can I ask why he was playing the *Fifth* – the passage from the finale. He answers that the Prince is planning to have it performed - although, just now, he has only one horn and no bassoons. Last year, Hans adds, he himself played *both* the viola and clarinet in the *Mass in C*. 'And sang at the same time, no doubt?' He smiles. I quiver again at his beauty. We are sitting a foot apart. I sense, too, that he likes me. His eyes glance over my lips, which I know are well-shaped, over the rounded flesh of my cheeks, from which my nose and chin, after all, come out straight and well. My own hair, with its dark, thick wave curls down over my collar.

'Do you play Mozart's concerto?' I ask. He shakes his head. Of course, Beethoven has pushed the memory of poor Mozart from the Prince's mind. 'Can *you*?' he asks, with a grin. He points the clarinet towards me. I take it warm from his hand, arrange my breath, and play the first few bars. When I return it, I put my hands over his, gazing frankly into his eyes.

'Put one finger here, one here: then this, and this, and this.' I place them on the keys.

He blows the first note, and I move the fingers: then a second, third, fourth, fifth and sixth time. I lie back and watch his fingers and his frown, as he seeks to repeat the sequence more smoothly, his lips around the reed; and my heart, like the music, flutters like a bird.

I am returning, sticky with heat, when I see the cook in her doorway, waving and calling in her stentorian voice: 'The Princess wants you: bring your fiddle. She wants music, she says.'

The West Wing ends in a circular tower reached by a narrow passage. Seen from the outside its pointed roof, rising behind the main façade, seems ready to float away. I have to drag myself up the narrow, winding stairs, pausing to notice the flicker of wings and the shrill cry of a swallow outside. From her boudoir up here the Princess can view the estate, but today her curtains are closed, and everything is dim. There are various knick-knacks, bits of china and bronze. In one corner there is a broken harpsichord, and in the other a suit of armour. The fireplace is hidden by a flower-patterned screen and oriental rugs are laid haphazardly across the floor.

The Princess, in her gold dressing-gown, reclines upon her green, silk-covered Recamier couch, in an attitude both restless and statuesque. Her small white feet are bare. There is one upright chair with arms, but far too narrow for me. She stares for a moment as if I were an intruder.

'Schuppenzall!' she exclaims, quite affably, 'You may sit at the end. She draws up her feet, and points. 'You like it?' she enquires, as I descend carefully, hoping that the bowed legs are stronger than they look. I tell her that I do. 'Ah, Schuppenzall, this couch belonged to my sister Elisabeth. The Count ordered it for her, all the way from Paris. Once we sat upon it together... the Count and the two of us. I remember the stained glass windows in her rooms, where his uncle lives now, when the sun was bright. Elisabeth liked the colours better than the garden outside... Ah, those were happier times. Do you know, we really thought that Bonaparte would be destroyed at Austerlitz... we thought we would visit Paris.' She halts herself abruptly and stiffens, remembering that I am a servant. 'You will play for me!' she says, severely, 'You, who did not play in church! Play me something different!' She forgets that I have played for her since I was a youth. In those days she was quite young, although even then they seemed to have been married forever. She galloped through the parks, jumping rose beds on her way.

Is there, I ask, as I check my strings, anything she wishes to hear? By different I know she means *not* Beethoven. She shakes her head and frowns. One has to pity her, I think: most of her own land gone in the wars, her husband a benevolent shell; and now Sophie, who must be ignored, constantly within her sight. So I start to play some Bach: the fuga of his third sonata. I turn my back and the Princess slips a little. They hardly know Bach in Vienna. The fuga: colossal, intricate. How long is it? Ten minutes? Now her toes are touching me. Weiss, of course, knows his Bach.

'Play it again!' she commands, rather hoarsely - and now her heels squirm and drum in rhythm against my spine. I play faster and faster to please her, and she responds with long, dry, sobbing gasps. As I play I sense the pressure of dark clouds building up outside. I think I hear a clap of thunder. The fuga twists and turns beneath my fingertips. When I finish and turn around the Princess is curled up sideways, apparently asleep.

***

The Count gives me a pouch of Italian leather with a hidden pocket for coins. Last year or the year before, he gave me that English telescope for which, he said, he had no further use. I keep it in my room in the palace, where I go to dream. He gives me the letters next: one for Prince Metternich, now officially Austrian foreign minister; the other for Beethoven. The air is cool and bright after an early morning shower. Down below us Sophie, in her apron, embraces her husband and son while the Count looks on with impatience. Hans and Weiss are to travel with me. Since it became known that Beethoven is organising a concert to raise money for the nuns of Baden, the Prince and Princess (she more than he) are eager to send musicians. I find that I am eager to go. The horses are brought round. The horses! The Count smiles at my expression. 'There is no carriage to spare,' he says. 'You will ride: two days, or three. Keep those letters safe.' If I see Herr Goethe, he adds, I am to mention that he, the Count, is making a translation into French and German of the new Russian poet, Pushkin, who deserves to be better known. There is a sample of translation in the pouch. I am to find out what Beethoven is writing, when he returns to Vienna, and what patrons he has. He will send for us all, to return to Vienna; the boy as well, he says. My horse (they tell me it is a pony) has steep glossy sides, which move. After a few attempts, aware that Hans is laughing with the others, I manage to hoist myself across its back. I can do this for Hans, and I can put my feet in the stirrups and let my horse follow his into a new world of wonders.

We pass mile on mile of orchards, fields, and forests hiding robbers. Sheep graze unattended, and the leaves are light and green. I never knew there were so many little birds in the world. Hans canters forward laughing, his golden head on fire, until he is out of sight and Weiss calls him anxiously back. The pony chafes my thighs.

We enter the shade of an oak wood: dappled, still, and yet more full of bird-song, where Hans trots ahead of us a little more circumspectly. Weiss has a map and compass. He sits a little hunched in the saddle with blithe and sparkling eyes, and tells me the names of birds.

It is evening when we emerge from the forest onto a post-road. Turning up it a little way, we find a stone that reassures us the road runs west to Prague and east to Breslau; and beyond it, half in the trees, we see what looks like an inn. There is a candle alight in the window. Moths flutter above a stream.

The place really is, or has been, an inn, and as we approach a woman comes out and bids us welcome. We sit out while our dinner is cooked, our bags upstairs on the one big bed, and Hans leans his head on my shoulder. I support him with a careful arm, and watch the moths flutter about, while Weiss points up at an owl giving a faint twitch to its wings.

After a dinner of rabbit stew, bread and wine, Weiss guides Hans upstairs to bed. The sturdy young man has suddenly faded back into a boy.

'Where's your husband?' I ask the woman, as she clears the plates.

'He is lying down, my lord.'

'Oh, and when does he work?'

'He cannot use his legs, my lord. They shot him in the back. Maybe he'd better have died. But he plants things, when it's warm, and he cleans the floors. Our wine is sent by his Colonel, thirty cases a year. Without that –' she turns her palm down. I take out a florin for another bottle of wine, looking at the scrubbed larch floor, and feeling suddenly stiff and badly chafed. Weiss comes in bright-eyed, humming the Allegretto of Opus 95, that halting, gleeful song of love. The woman returns with the wine and a bottle of schnapps.

'This for what you've paid, my lords. It's good schnapps though.'

'Oh!' says Weiss, bowing low, 'then you must drink with us!'

She is not unpleasant – puzzled, no doubt, by our manners, and our plain but well-made clothes. She sips, with a smile, from Hans's glass. Two of her upper teeth are missing, her nose is slightly flattened out, and her large brown eyes wander from gawping roundness to half-closed inattention and back. Weiss and I drink, and talk about the dynamics of the new quartet, humming an odd bar back and forth. Rough wine and schnapps never tasted so good, but Weiss's eyes are drawn to the woman, and she sees and smiles.

'My kind lords, another coin, or two…'

She lifts her smock up with one hand and lays one of her long breasts on the table as if it were a loaf. Weiss and I look at each other. He reddens, confused, but eager. I think of Mechthilt for a moment, then look at Weiss again and, tracing his likeness to Hans, I smile at him like a father, and toss out two more coins. They look at me gravely, inquiringly, before they turn and stretch out their palms to each other. I reach for the wine, and let them go. The darkness outside, still tinged with blue, covers the house in a cloak of silence, in which I hear my pony snuff as the back door opens. I get up and tiptoe down the passage towards it. I hear them now: they are in the hayloft; I can hear Weiss's quick, repeated groans. I think I hear the soldier snoring in the kitchen. Feeling sad and joyful at once I tiptoe upstairs in the darkness, lie down away from Hans in the bed, and wait for sleep to come. In the morning we have eggs, and take with us bread, cheese and wine. The woman smiles goodbye, but Weiss is looking away. We follow our track north and west through an uneventful day. Hans rides more slowly, in between me and his father, whose face is haggard and sickly. We cross a range of hills, coming up onto a plateau of rock and grass dotted with tiny flowers. There is a fine view from here of rolling forest and shining lakes and, in the distance, Weiss says, is Teplitz itself. As the sun goes down to our left I propose that we sleep in a beech wood. None of us desires to find another inn. We wrap ourselves in our cloaks, lie down in the grass and moss, and look up in silence at the canopy of leaves. High above a handful of stars appear and disappear. Early the following afternoon we are riding through orchards with the red-tiled roofs of Teplitz before us. A storm broke on the way, but the sun has dried us again.

We find our lodging-house and eat, and then I go straight out to deliver the letters, and to call on the Kapelmeister who, with Herr Polledro, is arranging the concert in Karlsbad for the burned nuns in Baden. We shall travel there by coach. Perhaps Beethoven will travel with us. Every street in Teplitz is lined with trees, allowing the sun to filter through in decent, measured quantities, but there does not seem to be a speck of dust. I see, among the grooms and servants, many Viennese, and in this clear, clean place, I feel more exposed and fatter than I ever do in Vienna. Mayseder's father is here, but there is no sign of Mayseder, and I have no time to spend in asking if he has been seen; here is the inventor, Malzel; here and there a Lobkowitz, or a Kinsky in his pomp; there are a number of officers - not required, it seems, to fight; over there a red-headed woman – Bettina Brentano, of course, but married now – on the arm of a gentleman of fifty: that, perhaps, is Goethe himself. I could ask her for the introduction that I need on the Count's behalf. Across the avenue I see the flaxen head of

Prince Metternich, trotting with Princess Bagration. I will
deliver the Count's letter to his secretary.

I find the quiet square I am seeking, and as I am looking
around for the house his friend, the sandy-haired merchant,
comes out with his daughter. They are dressed for riding; and
this, or their quiet air, makes me feel suddenly strange,
unnatural, half-human. Franz Brentano looks so decent, so
polished, and so ordinary. By contrast I am a centaur: dissolute
and still half-horse.

In the hallway I am hushed by Beethoven:

'Antonie has a headache, fool! Do not speak so loudly!' He
leads me up to the top floor, where the piano stands in a
corner, his writing desk by the window, and the door ajar to
the adjoining bedroom. We might be in Vienna, save that there
are no broken dishes, rags of clothes or bottles of wine. The
room is perfumed by a great vase of roses, and he himself
looks bright and fresh. He tells me the house is not rented, but
bought, as an investment. Next summer it will become another
lodging-house. I give him Rasumovsky's letter, wondering
about his great love, the beautiful, dark-eyed woman
downstairs who, I still believe, gives the joy and longing to
Opus 95. I am more sure than ever that it is so.

'Well.' he says at length, 'you must see Antonie, before you
go.'

I mention my meeting with Herr Polledro, and he is pleased:
'One must help the good sisters, always, for one's own sake
too – and there is plenty of money in this town.' He pauses
and looks at me darkly and directly: 'In addition,
Schuppanzigh, it gives me a reason for staying here; but all the
same my joy is slipping away. In two weeks Franz will take
Antonie back to Dresden, while I – ' He turns and picks
angrily at the piano. Over his shoulder he says: 'If the Count
really wants to know how I am *circumstanced* – then you
know!' 'The Count,' I say, 'still believes in your music. And
another new quartet, if you have one, would be good for us,
his musicians. I think we did justice to the Opus 95. ' 'You
know,' he says, 'there really should be a guild of musicians.
Instead of being the slaves of these Counts and Princes you

could ask a fair price for your work. If one of you is mistreated
– then the rest don't play!'

'That would be different,' I say, smiling. 'And then these
Counts could do what they liked. Let them play God in their
own affairs, and leave the music to us. But you can tell him
there is *no* music left in me. Only stray thoughts and dreams,
tending, if anything, towards another symphony, or perhaps
another Mass.'

Madame Brentano, her face etched with pain, summons up a
deep, reminiscent smile for me. She says she is better and calls
for coffee, but I cannot bear to stay; Beethoven's rapt,
delighted fondness is too much for a lonely fellow to bear.

As I walk back across the town I am struck by a fair-haired
man, a short, slender, attractive fellow, walking head-down
among the lordlings, looking completely forlorn. It might be
the picture of Young Werther. Then I come close and see it is
Weiss. His eyes have faded into an abyss of guilt. 'Come,' I
say to him, 'it was only natural.' He shakes his head
stubbornly. Then he looks about wildly at the silk dresses and
parasols, the glossy horses and the great array of uniforms, all
softened by the late sun. He hasn't bothered to change from
his dusty brown riding-clothes. 'Come on,' I say, 'to an inn.
They have their uses.' He shakes his head again. 'I keep
thinking,' he says, 'about Opus 95. I don't think I could play it
again. I am not worthy, Ignaz.' I pity Weiss's hurt. Lust, as I
know too well, only makes us feel the need for true affection
more. So he feels guilty, regardless of what he endures from
the Count and Sophie. Being unwilling to share my own
thoughts I leave my friend to the healing of time.

We have the first floor of a house, two bedrooms and a sitting-
room. Prices here in Teplitz are much the same as in Vienna.
When I return I find Hans sitting on the threadbare rug, gazing
at the small coal fire which casts the outer world into shadow.
The evenings here can turn quite cold. His shock of hair is like
a strange orb; a comet, bright on one side, streaming towards
my heart, as he looks up with troubled eyes. I pull up one of
the hard chairs and stretch my toes towards the grate. 'A
strudel for your thoughts,' I say. He gives half a smile: a

gleam. 'I was thinking of that girl,' he says, 'the one in the palace.'

'Do you mean what's-his-name – Fritz, the page-boy?'

'Yes, but I always knew it was a girl. We were sort of friends, though mother paid her more attention than me. She still does,' he adds bitterly. Ah, poor Hans! 'I would like to play like her – like the way you said she played – so I can play in Vienna. Will you teach me?' he asks. I stretch a hand towards him, then pause and nod. 'You're very nice,' he says. He edges his shoulder against my knee. 'Hans,' I say, 'I think it was only because that girl was in trouble. Your mother was helping her.'

'Hans – I'm sick of being Hans; and I'm so tired of Prince Lichnowsky, and Gratz, and the other boys!'

'But has no-one told you?' I say. 'Ah, perhaps the Count had only just decided. You are coming back to Vienna.' He looks up at me and smiles, still half disbelieving. He shakes, and I lay my hand gently on his hair, his bright red hair; and suddenly he throws himself against my shaking heart, and into my loving, deep, and much too fat, embrace.

***

With regret, I have sold our horses: I will never forget our ride. I am sorry, too, that Russia has lost this war. I have as little time for Bonaparte as does Beethoven, who leaves Karlsbad just as Rasumovsky arrives there, with Therese. The Count spends a morning in discussion with Prince Metternich. The mood among the nobility is one of quiet despair, but these have been sweet weeks for me. Gentle love of Hans has so contented, so sated me that I have no more to ask for as we travel home in one carriage. Every moment of the concert I was thrilled for him. There is no music now: only the rumble of wheels and the beating of hooves outside, making it hard to tell what the Count is thinking, while the four of us keep up a respectful silence. He leans back in his corner, apparently at ease.

At a more prosperous type of inn he calls for wine: plain, rough, country wine. He drinks and eats with us. In the next room some peasants play rough, lilting country tunes, which cause us all to smile.

The Count, in his English jacket, seems smaller and more jovial. Therese, who is dressed simply but quite well, beats her foot to the tune. She and Weiss catch each other's eye, and start to mime together another melody, not unlike the peasants', but with trills that seem misplaced. I watch their fingers on their imaginary scrolls, and after a while I catch it – a snatch of the *Pastoral*. Where did she pick that up? I think of Beethoven, glowering at our hands in Karlsbad, to see mistakes in tempo that his ears no longer catch, and then I notice that the Count is also watching Weiss and the girl, as if there was something he disliked; but when the girl looks, not boldly, but still straight at him, with a pursed-up grin like Linke's, he grins back and raises his glass. Once again Weiss cannot take his eyes from Therese, but it is no more, and no less, than a quiet sympathy.

In the carriage the Count was holding carefully on his knee a shiny dark-green, plump-leaved plant, of a sort I did not recognise. 'A cactus,' he said, when he saw me looking, 'a plant that grows in the desert.' As I go up to my own room, I see through the Count's open door the cactus now putting out its bright red flowers – really amazing bright blood red, and I see that the leaves are covered with little thorns, and it occurs to me that it is a gift for Sophie, one that speaks of all that cannot be helped. 'Here,' it says to me, 'this here – yes, this – is what love is.'

Third Quartet: Winter 1814

9. Mayseder (21st December)

Three of us are standing under a new glass roof in the
ballroom. 'But Talleyrand…' The Princess shudders: 'How
can *he* be here?'
'Ah, poor France!' says Count Rasumovsky, making France
sound like an indigent relative, or perhaps an ailing mistress.
No-one knows how Talleyrand managed to gain entry to the
Congress, from which France was meant to be excluded, but
the Count, as ever, appears philosophical.
In the twenty-three years that I have been alive, one French
king was executed, and another is now restored. Bonaparte is
exiled to Elba. Russia is triumphant, and all the junkers of
Europe are in full cry. Life is full of shattered hopes, among
which I must pick my way, through the Congress of Vienna (it
has been four months already); through the palace, where Karl
has a way of appearing unexpectedly; through the demands of
the Viennese princes in their town mansions and through the
Russians, the Prussians, and even the Italians, in their hotels or
borrowed houses, asking for a musician to give them a silly
song or an improvised waltz. Vienna is the home of music and
so, along with the formal concerts, in every salon in which the
political non-happenings and rumours are discussed, there
must be a little music as balm for tired brains. The English,
though, keep to themselves.
A few such small gatherings have taken place at the
Rasumovsky palace, in the library, or in the Canova room; but
the Count (promoted to Prince, but no-one remembers) is
almost fully occupied with his leading role in the talks, and is
also preparing the greatest ball of the season, for which has
been built this extension to his ballroom, transparent to reveal,
in the watches of the night, a latticework of frost and a host of
shining stars. It is a mainly wooden structure, the far wall

having completely gone, except for two pillars of brick to hold the long roof-timbers. In its place are two new glass doors, and through them, as in a peepshow, one may see a little cottage. Behind its little fence Franz Weiss's leeks are earthed up to their necks.

'But it is cold!' says the Princess, shuddering once more. The Count points to a hole, partway up the structure. That, he explains, is where the hot air will come in, brought by a pipe from the main system. His uncle, who is gifted in such matters, is supervising the work. Here, beneath the glass, is where the musicians will play: and of course after the dancing – the Count looks at me with a wry, familiar look – the Rasumovsky string quartet will perform for the cognoscenti, but – the Princess has raised this point – those who wish can continue supper or wander where they will. The Count has hinted that it will be our last public performance: five years was the term he intended to maintain us. Well, it will be in front of men who are the stuff of legend: Talleyrand, the Tsar of Russia, our own Prince Metternich, and many other heads of state, ministers and courtesans. With ten days to go, and Christmas in between, this ball is still the talk of Vienna. Meanwhile the Princess (a kind of diplomat too) goes to the social gatherings in her black silk dress, and I go with her in case some music should be required. Now and again Madame Ertmann and I, coming in separately, combine in the Spring sonata. Every night a different salon: a Kinsky, a Lobkowitz; but it is said by some that the Countess Erdody's little apartment is where the most interesting things are to be heard. There is sympathy for the good Princess's loss (Prince Lichnowsky – heart attack), and great astonishment at how handsome she looks. Every night the Karnthenor, since the Tsar himself attended, is nearly full for Beethoven's *Fidelio*. Its heroine, Leonore, the wife who dresses up as a pageboy, now stands for freedom from the tyranny of the French. The erstwhile French Empress, Marie-Louise, is also restored to the Hapsburgs. The trumpets arriving are Russia, Bonaparte is sent to Elba, and Europe is unchained in an orgy of peace and joy.

There is, I hear, a sort of rival to me – a female virtuoso who plays in other great houses, entrancing her hearers there with mere fragments of Mozart and Bach. Some think that a woman who plays the violin must be quite improper, gypsy-like, but she is said to come of decent family. She is a novelty, and she has the backing of Schuppanzigh, Archduke Rudolph, and Count Rasumovsky, all of whom claim that her playing is unsurpassed. And, very cleverly, she has styled herself 'Leonore'.

The Princess had sent for me on her way to the ballroom, and on her way back to her rooms she sends me off across town with a note for the banker, Salomon Rothschild who, ironically, is renting the Lichnowsky town-house. In spite of the quiet life of his later years, the dead Prince left extensive debts. The streets are as cold as the ballroom, under a swathe of broken cloud, but over the marble door where the Congress meets, in the Bundeskanzleramt, there are patches of sun like golden coins.

I have known the Lichnowsky house since I was a child, when Salieri, my teacher then, showed me Beethoven coming out. Now I am shown upstairs to a waiting room, and there, before me, is Linke, who gives me his most sardonic grin. I explain, in a whisper, that I am here on behalf of Princess Lichnowsky. Without his cello Linke looks small and tough, with silver streaks in his hair. He grins his badger's grin again: 'Always waiting for someone, aren't we? Here we are in the same old town – you, Beethoven, Count Rasumovsky - still here. Even the Frenchman is back.' I presume he means Ramballe, whom I have also seen, walking with Talleyrand, the French ambassador. 'It seems,' I say, rather cautiously, 'that the past is past with you.' Since the summer of 1812 I have lived at my father's and kept away from my fellow-musicians as much as possible. We have not played many quartets: Rasumovsky has often been away – even as far as France.

Linke seems disinclined to reply but, in any case, we find that we are being watched by Rothschild himself, who has come noiselessly in. He ushers us into his office, which was once the drawing room (in fact the grand piano still stands there in the corner), and motions us to his desk. His dress, down to the dark silk waistcoat, is immaculate.

'Since you are friends and colleagues,' he remarks, 'I am sure you will not object if I see you together. Besides, time saved in business…' He holds out his hand for the bag which Linke has drawn from under his coat and weighs it in his bony hand. Then he turns his head and looks at me from one side of his nose. I feel his gaze on my new clothes, and I remember how I first met him, when I was dressed in the Count's red livery, as I shall be once more. Now half the Congress owes him money, but he is discreet. 'One hundred florins to be added to our account,' says Linke, anxiously. 'Here!' Salomon Rothschild thrusts the bag at me. 'But you must tell the Princess this is a gift, out of respect. I will be happy to lend, if more is required.' 'That's generous,' growls Linke. Rothschild, with a stately bow, motions us to sit down. I balance the weight of coin on my knee, feeling I am just a lackey, while Linke, peasant-like, struggles to see his earnings – I suppose really his niece's, that is Leonore's earnings – treated in such a fashion. Rothschild writes him a receipt. 'As I have said to you both before,' remarks the banker, 'I am happy to be of service to you gentlemen. I admire your gifts. But, like me, you need to cultivate your friends. Herr Beethoven, who takes no such trouble, is very fortunate that the Archduke Rudolph protects him. You also need more friends and protectors of the right sort, just as I need the good will of Princess Lichnowsky, who can talk to her friends about this proposal to Congress from Herr Gentz.' What Herr Gentz puts forward, of course, Prince Metternich has already approved. 'What proposal?' I ask him impatiently. What friends should I cultivate? How can this fellow, a Jew after all, be of other use to me? 'There is a proposal,' he says, 'to have our people equal.' He straightens his back, puts his hands behind him, and fixes us with his gaze: 'Jews to be equal: equal with you.' 'Ah', says Linke, 'I see your drift; and Count Rasumovsky?' Rothschild shakes his head and says, with perfect detachment: 'All Russians, my friend, are Jew-killers. I do not expect his support.'

Within a few yards of the house we see Karl coming towards

us. I shudder. He makes us both a mock bow, then points to me and to the Princess's carriage, inviting me to enter. I suddenly lose my temper and thrust the coin into his hands. 'Here!' I say, 'you take it to her. I am going to walk.' He takes the bag without any comment and goes.

Linke and I walk on, taking in the bustle. For two months now all the streets have been full of carriages: carriages at first bedecked with the red and yellow of fallen leaves; now in the morning carriages that glitter white with frost. The shop-windows gleam more brightly, and the Nymphen have new frocks. Just for the moment all of Vienna is clear and bright, and in spite of Karl, in spite of all my fears, I cannot help feeling young and hopeful. I am only twenty-three.

I notice that I have adjusted my walking-pace to Linke's limp. We pass the Stepansdom, where more carriages are waiting. Their owners, perhaps, are at Mass. Sitting in a closed barouche, alone, and looking straight ahead, is Captain Ramballe. He sits there in his greatcoat and hat, and does not move. It scarcely seems possible that he is the same man, but then two years past we thought the French had conquered Russia, and sometimes, among all people, there is still disbelief that Bonaparte is gone.

A cartload of sacks of wheat swings across our path, into the gate of the Lobkowitz palace. Urchins with little bowls race after some fallen grains. Linke reaches into a small bag at his belt, and scatters some silver and copper onto the stones. They eddy, for a moment, like a flock of feeding birds, before they begin to pick up grain and coin together.

We turn off into a side-street. I have no thought of where I am going. It's a long time, I think, since I've seen Beethoven. I used to understand him, a little. I have a copy –my father bought it – of *Opus 95*, the quartet. A strange piece it is, especially after the beauties of the '*Harp*'. Anyway, all they want from him now is *Fidelio*, and mighty tunes. Linke shakes his head when I ask if *he* has seen him. There's a lot I'd like to ask him – Linke, that is – such as how he manages not to seem beholden to anyone much. I suppose the answer is that he lives in the present: a peasant in his mentality as well as his looks.

My own dream is freedom still. If mankind cannot be free, I at least desire to stand alone, and to be a true composer, and not to wear a livery.

As if he could read my thoughts, he asks me if I've finished my sonata: it is promised for a soirée at the Countess Erdody's next week. I assure him it will be ready. Of all of our patrons, I remark, Countess Erdody has aged the most; but of course she has always been frail. He begins to walk faster, limping, hands in pockets, along a street so narrow the cobbles still bear traces of ice. Then he halts, and says that I am wrong: the Count and Sophie have aged the most. I realise we are standing right outside his apartment. Because I was not thinking I have come out of my way, but I can easily find my way back to the palace again. Everything in this area seems much smaller than when I came here with him, so many years ago. Linke opens the street door and seems about to speak again; but in the end he raises his hand, and closes it in my face.

***

My sonata for clarinet, commissioned by Princess Lichnowsky, is in fact far from finished. I cannot write it at home, where my sisters have turned the house into a milliner's; but the palace, though sometimes quiet, is equally distracting. Tension seems to grip it as never before. There is the Princess herself and there is also Karl, fixing me, when he sees me, with an uncompromising stare. So it is reluctantly that I go back there, where I have my little room on the ground floor, the same one that was once occupied by Linke. The attics these days have as many servants as they can hold.

I am almost safely there when Sophie calls to me from the library. She motions me to take a seat, closes the door and glances all around her, even up at the balcony where all the rows of books tower into darkness. The whole room is as dim as a forest. The sun outside has completely disappeared. She sits down opposite me in an armchair as if the room belonged to her, and yet still clearly listening out for any sign of disturbance. Her legs, with that swollen foot, are apart and uncrossed, her hands moving in her lap.

I ask her where I can find young Hans. I have the clarinet part, first movement, ready for him to learn. Sophie shakes her head. Then she adds that he mostly goes about with Schuppanzigh, but that she will let him know. I tell her I must get to work, but she leans forward and fixes me with something of her old look, green and fierce, but also more troubled than I remember. The rest of her face looks unhealthy and there is a fold under her chin.

'Don't you want to marry?' she says. I shake my head.

'Consider it,' she says quickly, 'you and Therese, both young musicians. Your future would be assured, the Princelings would want to hire you; with a husband she might continue to play the violin – in their salons, that is.'

I am astonished. 'Come,' she says urgently, 'you are not promised elsewhere?' I shake my head and then I tell her: 'It is impossible.' For I believe that Karl would murder me. I am sure that he has other plans for 'Leonore'. It makes me close my eyes, but when I do I see Therese's little jig, and her remote face looking somewhere else, and it seems as if she has three jigging pairs of arms and legs.

Sophie has been watching me. 'Think it over,' she says. 'Let me arrange it, while I still can.'

'But why,' I ask, and then, as it strikes me, 'is it the Count's idea?'

'I did her wrong,' Sophie replies. 'That is one reason. And why should you not marry her? There are reasons why you should! No it is not the Count's idea, but let me get his blessing for you both, and do not wait!'

Could I marry her? What would they say: Linke – my father – Princess Lichnowsky?

'But if I cannot love her?' I ask.

'Ah, you can learn to love. That is what people do.' There is half a smile on her mouth, although her eyes are bitter and full of tears.

At this moment we hear, beyond the door, the dim noise of hammer on metal. It makes us jump.

'Ah, the old fool!' Sophie exclaims, 'the evil one!'

It is Peter Andreyich, of course, working on the flue from the kitchen. It is the old man's only occupation now, and thinking that Karl is probably with him I jump up and leave her, thinking that I must get out of the palace at any cost. But as I am in the corridor the banging stops, and Peter Andreyich shuffles past me without a glance. Thankfully I enter my little room and close the door. I sit down at once and begin to write, looking up at the Noah's dove and making the most of the light which slants halfway across my page. I write on and on, refusing now to think of anything else.

I manage to work for an hour, and then, as I was half-expecting, Natalie slips into the room and draws me across to the bed. We make love in silence, and I am certainly ready to squeeze those plump white breasts, to tickle and thrust as she has taught me ever since the first time she came in here with a tray from the kitchen.

We fall asleep, and when I wake the light has nearly drained away. From beyond the oak partition there comes again the sound of tapping and then I hear voices, and suddenly someone speaks very loudly in French. Natalie stirs awake. I put my hand over her mouth. There happens to be a little knot-hole in this partition, just at the side of the bed, and by sliding carefully onto my knees I can put my eye to it while Natalie silently puts a blanket over my shoulders. Next door a candle sits on the floor, and I can see one of Peter Andreyich's ears, as he stoops down, until the leg of a pair of yellow breeches obscures him from view, and then I know that the voice I heard belongs to Metternich.

'Splendid!' says Metternich quietly now, in German. 'The Tsar will have to acknowledge him. Are you sure the old man agrees?'

'Certainly he does,' replies Karl's surly voice. 'I have shown him the uniform he is to wear: that of Russia in Catherine's time.'

'And Rasumovsky knows nothing?'

Of course not. He is too busy. Our Count will look like a fool.'

'A fool he was,' says Metternich, 'to try and make a fool of me, with his composer, and his talk of masters and mistresses.'

Karl's hand picks up the candle, and all three of them depart. As we get dressed I whisper to Natalie what I have heard.

'Shall I tell Madame Sophie,' she asks, 'so that she can tell the Count?'

'No,' I say, 'we don't understand it. And she might do something foolish.' At this Natalie nods. 'We must be silent,' I add. We must never let Karl guess that we have overheard. It is no surprise to me that they are plotting against the Count; yet, from what I know of the Congress, Rasumovsky is in the ascendant, Metternich precarious. It is rumoured that the Tsar wants Metternich dismissed.

I light a candle and try to return to my work, until the great clock in the corridor chimes seven. Then, quickly washed and brushed, I go to the Princess's rooms. Natalie smiles at me as she stands and brushes the Princess's long black mane, and the Princess smiles too. She is restive, talkative. We are, she declares, to have our fill of pleasures in this Christmas season, this Christmas Congress season of balls. After so many, she smiles, she still adores a ball. They say that by the New Year all treaties will have been agreed. Afterwards – she pauses, looks at us both, and nods – it may be best for all if she stays here in Vienna and marries the Count. She believes that her poor dear sister would have approved. All her friends, such as the Kinskys, and even Prince Metternich, would welcome the Count among them; he has long been as Austrian as he is Russian, and really her oldest friend even though, just lately, she has scarcely been able to see him... 'And you, young fellow,' she looks at me appreciatively, 'you should be married too!' She is gay, and hardly looks fifty. When she takes off her robe and Natalie puts her into her dress her high shoulders are smooth and white, and she smells sweetly of roses and jasmine. Black silk, with pearls and a plain silver band, lend elegance to her long, white arms. In the carriage, wrapped in her furs, she leans against me and smiles to herself.

***

The public rooms of the Palais de Princes have been redecorated in the blues and golds of French Monarchy. The fireplaces blaze with logs, mirrors and chandeliers abound, and the newest and largest types of couches are everywhere. Here there are no dungeons. I stand with my fiddle ready, and

I am not afraid, as I take my place among the lesser mortals. 'Herr Mayseder. Once again…' – Salomon Rothschild is not the least surprising of Prince Metternich's guests - made up, on the female side, by his wife, the Princess Bagration and Duchess Wilhemine de Sagan. These last two are his rival mistresses. All three look like china dolls next to Princess Lichnowsky. I know few of the male guests, apart from Rothschild and Zmeskall, who now introduces me to a small, bald fellow; a smiler with yellow teeth. This is a Russian, Bi-li-bin, who is in the retinue of Rasumovsky's deputy, Count Nesselrode, who is lodged with the Tsar at Schonnbrunn. The Russian delegation is so large, he explains, because so many of them wished to come and see our famous ambassador, Rasumovsky, since he is never to be seen in Saint Petersburg. He is charmed to meet a member of his famous string quartet. He is pleased, he says, looking around, to see that the Prince has not invited any Frenchmen tonight. France is finished, after all, and the Tsar fails to see why they are represented at all, or what Prince Metternich or, indeed, Count Rasumovsky, can possibly have to say to them.

At this point I am called upon to play. Madame Ertmann and I (she is here, she is everywhere, always with the Major hard by and upright as a tuning-fork), perform the Spring Sonata again. No-one these days objects to a little well-worn Beethoven. His latest work, as Zmeskall is explaining as I return, is a somewhat different matter, as he modestly admits the dedication of that strange quartet to himself, and recounts to us the strange sensation it made at the Countess Erdody's, when its troubled nature seemed, to him at least, to echo all the madness and turbulence of 1812; and how this was then made stranger by the unheard-of choice of a female 'primo', the young lady now known as 'Leonore'. It will be fascinating, he thinks, to hear it again, with the same players, at the same salon in two days' time, and see if the effect is the same. And, he adds urbanely, he also looks forward to hearing my own new composition, which is bound to be graceful. 'Leonore', Zmeskall adds, is much admired; and he can see no harm himself in her playing duets with Schuppanzigh or Linke,

respected musicians in Prince Rasumovsky's employ.
I look across the room and see my Princess, like a statue,
wrapped in her own imperious thoughts.
'Ah, Count Rasumovsky,' Bi-li-bin exclaims, in his tinny
French, 'so Russian still in his habits! To take up with a
peasant dame, like one of our country gentlemen, and have
people wondering where he keeps his bastards; and all the
while his old father still running about the place...'
'You mean the man they call his uncle...?'
'Is his father, of course!'
Bi-li-bin looks around to see who might be listening, and then
proceeds to tell us a story.
'This old man and his brother were both favourites of
Catherine the Great. The brother, Peter, the Count's uncle,
died at home in the Ukraine many years ago. One morning in
1765 this man, whose true name is Kyril, Rasumovsky's
father, went off hunting but, by some strange oversight, he left
the Empress tied to her bed and unable to free herself. Not
until hours later, when they dared to disturb her, was she freed
by her maids. When Papa Rasumovsky returned he was sent
into exile, but not before Catherine had hot lead poured into
his ears. Completely deaf, of course, he wandered into Italy;
and there, eventually, was reunited with his son, our present
Count, whose own career, begun in the navy, had not been
affected by his father's misfortune. From Rome and Naples
the Count, by this time a great man in his own right, and with
his fortune no doubt enhanced by his father's remaining
wealth, settled here with his paintings and statues.
'But the absurd thing,' Bi-li-bin concludes, 'would be to
suppose that the Tsar has any concern at all with this relic! '
'Indeed,' chuckles Zmeskall, 'he must be older than
Talleyrand himself!'
'For whom,' answers Bi-li-bin, 'the Count also shows a
strange consideration. One wonders what hold that old devil
has.'
Suddenly, to my horror, I see that Metternich, with his chilly
face, is coming towards me with the Princess on his arm. Of
what, I think, shall I be accused? His three ladies look on at

me with distant contempt. Just before he has reached me, as if moved by clockwork, Rothschild steps forward, bows, and offers Princess Lichnowsky a scroll of paper. He has, he says, acquired it by error. Will the Princess, as a patron of music, return it with his compliments, to Count Rasumovsky? The Princess unrolls it and looks at the cover.

'Good heavens – a quartet – by Andrei!'

'Does he,' asks Metternich smoothly, 'add composition to all his other talents?'

And suddenly Herr Gentz, Bi-li-bin, Zmeskall and the three distant graces smile at her with dry compassion.

The Princess throws up her head for a moment, rolling her eyes around the room. She glances at me and the fiddle, but thinks better of it. It has been a charming evening. She will convey Prince Metternich's greetings to the Count.

***

There is a sharp, dry cold in the carriage. The Princess leans against me, holding the roll of paper. Odours of musk and violet in the black fur she wears seem to lighten her body's pressure. When we arrive at the palace – watched from the box by Karl – I bow to her as she puts her foot on the great cascade of the staircase and, getting no response, turn away from her slowly and leave her to her meditations; but as I approach my room once more, I hear her steps behind me in the corridor, smell once more the waft of perfume and feel her breath on my neck. I think, for a moment, she is going to the library, which is always lit; but as I enter my little room she follows me inside and sits herself down on the bed. I hasten to light a candle. The room is cold. I have no fire. She motions me to lock the door. Then she sits quite still for a moment, before unrolling the manuscript.

'Quartet…1809…' She looks up. 'You have seen this?' I nod. I played first and Fritz played second, with Linke and Weiss; but no Schuppanzigh to judge it. There was Sophie and there was the Count. There was Peter Andreyich, who that Russian fellow claims is really the Count's own father. And then in came Beethoven, with that wondrous new quartet, 'The Harp'. And afterwards the Princess commanded me to write a polka.

Now she motions me to sit by her, and hold up the candle. She reads the bars to half-way down, as if she would uncover some secret. She scans the rest and turns the page. Then, hunching her shoulders, she throws back her head and says: 'It's no good, then. They hate him!' She and her husband, I have heard, knew every note of Beethoven's first six quartets. Schuppanzigh once told me that that music, almost forgotten now, rivalled Mozart and Haydn. So a glance has told her that what is here is third-rate: the attempt, of course, of a man who has never studied composition. And Rothschild, or Gentz, or Metternich will know it too. They will have summoned someone – Salieri, perhaps – to give them his opinion. 'They hate him!' she exclaims again, 'and I – I cannot help him – he has never confided in me… and look here!' I lean forward. In the top corner is one word, which I cannot remember having seen, and that word is 'Sophie'.
'He will never give up that woman who, with her husband, must be planning…'
No, Princess,' I say, 'she loves him in good faith.' I am still holding the candle in its dish, which lights up nothing except the page and the dim white dove in the window. I am sitting beside the Princess on the bed. My leg is touching hers but I do not move it away; I can sense that she likes it there. A cold draught catches my ankles.
'Yes, I know,' she answers sadly. 'I have always known. But – can it be right?'
Can it be right to fall in love? My arm is touching her back. She turns and looks at me with her dark, timid eyes. 'I am not – young,' she says. I look into her face and tighten my hold. Suddenly I am in love. She throws the pages away from her, making the candle gutter and fail. I bend to put it on the floor and feel the fur slip from her shoulders. As I recover her long white arms bring my head onto her bosom, all roses and jasmine, and then with a shuddering breath she bends her head and finds my mouth. When I enter her in darkness, always stroking to keep her warm, I cannot help believing that I am almost safe.

10. Linke (26-28 December)

'Why on earth,' I ask Therese, 'did you sell - to Salomon Rothschild, of all people - Rasumovsky's dreadful score? What if he should find out?'

It is the day after Christmas -1814 - but Christmas is forgotten this year. They keep the Vienna Congress instead, treating the day as no more than a pause in its glittering whirl, laced with the never-ending gossip and rumour about the Count. It was only yesterday that Anna confessed the sale to me.

Therese looks up from the ottoman, resting her chin on the fiddle that I kept for her during those long months in 1812, until the Count brought her home. There is a sudden green or yellow spark in her eyes. She smiles, and plays a phrase or two of Bach. The way she jigs about sometimes shows that she's not right in the head, but playing always soothes her a little, as it still soothes her little boy, to whom she has played and played ever since she came back, and we found she was pregnant. Of course I get no answer to my question. According to Anna, Rothschild came and offered to buy it. But how should he even know the Count had written a string quartet? How, on the other hand, should he not? The palace is always full of spies. I was away in Hungary, with Maria, last spring - 1813. Therese was expecting the child. The Cossacks were marching east, and I think the Count was away. Everyone was short of money, fearful that the war in Prussia would spread; no-one wanted a new gown, or even an alteration. If Anna were to speak her mind, I think she might say that I was partly to blame.

It is true that I had already had dealings with Rothschild myself, taking out a small loan on Maria Erdody's behalf. However, I now believe that it was really Therese's idea to sell her copy which, unbeknown to me, she had brought with her when she left the palace. I remember how she was forced to play it with Mayseder, Weiss and I in that frightful atmosphere; Beethoven, Sophie, the Count all mad and Peter Andreyich shaking his head. She had made the copies herself – if the Count were to remember! It was her first day in the palace, and she has never forgotten the terror and confusion that she had to hide beneath her boy's disguise. Perhaps, in her muddled way, this is an act of revenge; or perhaps she wanted to get rid of it, though how Rothschild got involved is still a mystery. But no-one could have guessed at the consequences. I have heard that someone, at a Lobkowitz gathering, hummed his own tune behind the Count's back.

Luckily the Count has little time to dwell on such things, and in any case the air is full of private gossip. Yesterday I heard of fisticuffs between Prince Metternich's mistresses; no doubt spiteful things are said about Maria Erdody. So busy has the Count been that since the Congress began the Rasumovsky quartet has not been summoned by him until tonight. It is, Schuppanzigh has said, another wholly private, one might indeed say secret performance, of Opus 59, number 3 - one more dose of the drug for him, snatched from his long hours of duty; at the same time a preparation for our public performance after the ball, which may well be our last. This summons now fills me with a strange foreboding. I think of the dark second movement; the thrum in it as of a lost, enquiring and uncertain soul.

I last saw the Count in early autumn, when the smells of crushed grapes and apples were wafting into the city. The Congress was full of excitement and bustle, hope and expectation, whereas now the diplomats look gloomy, and seem at best to be nursing the flame, just as Anna and I huddle around our little fire. I was in the Director's office in the Karnthenor, where we had just rehearsed *Fidelio*, and Beethoven was there, looking through the score. In walked Rasumovsky and nodded to us both. In his usual way he congratulated Beethoven, saying that the Tsar would be astonished by the music, as well as delighted by the triumph over evil. The Tsar is, of course, a deeply religious man. Beethoven laid his quill across the page, looked up half-bewildered as though he had not heard (and perhaps he had not), and then growled that his music was against *every* tyranny. In addition to which, he added, speaking as if the Count was not there, it was about a marriage, of proper and perfect love. They faced each other, the Count in frockcoat and cravat, his face devoid of specific purpose, and Beethoven newly turned-out except for a blob of ink on his cuff. It seemed to me that they were absorbed in two sides of one mystery.

'Let us not judge each other,' said the Count at last. 'I have been listening to the rehearsal. I admit that in the past I thought your opera too much of a fairy-tale. But now – I cannot tell you how much it contents me.' Once more Beethoven looked bewildered, and then in a voice of alarm, but with a sudden smile in his eyes, he shouted: 'I don't judge you, sir!' Again I wondered how much he had heard. But now the Count looked lost and confused, until, as if to restore him, Beethoven began to ask him questions: Must the French have back their king? Will Bonaparte stay on Elba? What will happen to Poland, and to Italy? I do not remember the answers: only that, in the end, they shook hands.

Maria Erdody has asked if I would live in Hungary as tutor to her children. Much as she wants to be in Vienna, she misses them and Hungary and she longs to go back. Her husband continues to travel. I try to picture continuous life with her: sometimes hopping along like a blackbird, other times swift and deft as a wren. I could send enough money to Anna and Therese. The little Countess is not like other aristocrats: she does not consider herself to be of a higher species. But I have also thought of going back to Breslau with Anna, now that we are no longer poor, and making what living I can. I could still visit Vienna, just as in the old days. I should be dependent on no-one. Life is easy with either of them, which makes it hard to choose; only, in either case, Therese and the child are a problem to be solved.

I come to the palace in the late afternoon, long before we have to perform, in order to find Schuppanzigh, who I believe is resting upstairs. I have something more to ask him about Opus 95 – a passage that I still don't understand. I go first to leave my cello in the library, which is empty. I can explain my problem without it. Then, before I begin the long climb up to the attics, I look inside the Canova room, and I see Sophie dusting the statues. She applies her cloth with careful detachment to the genitals of Apollo; then, when she turns to move on, she hobbles with an air of cautious, heavy abstraction. And suddenly I feel her misery pervade the room, like a cold white vapour. What would her old friend Beethoven say if he could see her now? I turn away, with ice in my heart.

Schuppanzigh is leaning on the windowsill. As I open the door he turns and puts a finger to his lips. Young Hans is asleep on the bed. He motions me to sit on the chair, takes the score out of my hand and, as always, begins to smile when he scans the first few bars. Then, with a little hesitation, he awakens Hans by ruffling his fine red hair, and tells him to go downstairs: he should be looking for Herr Mayseder. Hans looks angry, but sees me and goes. Ignaz sits down on the bed, looks at the score and sighs. I explain the problem, but for once he has no answer. He suggests I ask my niece. I already have. But, as he knows, her playing is pure instinct. Schuppanzigh frowns. 'All I can say is do it your way, from first to last. Like a heart missing beats – isn't that the way it is?'

What bothers me is a passage in the Allegretto – do I emphasise a harshness, which is there, or echo the melancholy of Weiss's viola? Do it your way – that's not so easy. I no longer trust my instincts; rather, every note I play could be a step in the wrong direction.

'The Count gave it to me,' says Ignaz. I have been looking at a strange object, a telescope on a brass tripod, pointing upwards at the rapidly darkening sky. 'You can see right into the fields,' says Ignaz, 'through that gap, past old Birkenstock's house. You can see into their drawing-room, as if you were outside the window - but, of course, it isn't right to pry.'

There are still three hours to go. Anna and Therese are sitting quietly at home. Maria, too, will be sitting by her fire, glad of a quiet evening. I had thought vaguely of calling in on Weiss, but instead I find myself in the servant's room opposite to

Schuppanzigh's, the very room once occupied by Therese, where now I lie on the bed and doze in Natalie's arms. Gobbets of frost from last night cling to the window-pane – there has been no sun today – and Natalie pulls the blankets up to our chins. I lean against her, purely for warmth, and tell her how I saw Sophie dusting the statues downstairs. Natalie clicks her tongue.

'Madame Sophie is meant to be resting,' she says. 'I am looking after her. She is not to run about.'

'Except,' I say, 'to Countess Erdody's.' It is agreed that she will serve at Maria's soirée tomorrow. She and Anna are both required. And then, the day after tomorrow, it will be Sophie's birthday, and Maria has asked her to come as her guest in the afternoon.

Very well,' says Natalie, 'she goes to your friend the Countess, but otherwise she must rest.' Her tone makes me wonder. Also, when I look at her, there are suddenly crows' feet around her eyes. I ask her to tell me, truly, how she came to the palace. It was twenty years ago, she says, during the Revolution, when she left Paris and came here with nothing. She was a kitchen-girl, and then a maid to the dead Countess. She remembers the palace being built. She remembers laying the Countess out. Perhaps – she chuckles easily – people suppose her to be une émigrée – a royalist: but no, she believed in liberty, equality; liberty of all kinds. She had a lover, older than her, until he got jealous and hurt her with a broken bottle. Then her friend Olympe de Gouge wrote a statement of women's rights: "women, unfold the energy of your bodies, and you will see these men, your servile adorers, proud to share with you the treasures of the Revolution."

'And what happened then?' I ask.'Oh, of course the Jacobins cut off her head. When I came here first I did not care what happened to me. Everyone I knew was dead. And now Madame Sophie reminds me of Olympe. Her feelings are very strong.'

The fire burns, the candles are lit, and the velvet curtains are drawn across the library windows. The four of us assemble in silence. Schuppanzigh broods heavily. Mayseder has dark patches under his eyes. Weiss, rabbit-like as ever, lets his glance dart about; he looks, as usual, forlorn.

The Count enters, as always, in his Persian dressing-gown; and with him come Peter Andreyich, and – not Sophie but Therese! Judging by his sideways glance, Peter Andreyich approves of her. Her hair is dyed black, and in her ears are long drops of pure, honey-coloured gold. The dress shows her ankles above a pair of ruby slippers. Her face is like a mask, except for the eyes. Schuppanzigh, I think, might have warned me. Anna, too, might have told me. I suppose it is like the Count.

Flames from the logs, which are studded with little pieces of coal, flicker orange, yellow and blue. The candles drip light and wax, and Peter Andreyich strains his watery eyes. Therese wears red silk that presses down on her like a cocoon, and she does not move.

Tonight there is a different manner to their listening, as if it really might be a very first or a very last time. The Count sighs audibly, as if he were letting it go. Therese blinks as I pluck the bass string, just as Sophie used to do. Weiss inclines his head to her as he opens the minuet. Peter Andreyich looks different: uglier, if possible. Still, his attention does not waver: his concentration speaks to us even though we know, as everybody does these days, that he is completely deaf.

The fire leaps up and makes dappled shadows on the books, blotches like a panther's skin. Nothing moves but our fingers and bows, and flames like the tongues of beasts. Leaning back a little to help me concentrate I look up and see Sophie, in a morning-gown, standing on the balcony just above us, and looking down at the Count. I cannot see her expression, which I fear will be one of torment and rage; but when she turns her eyes to us she sees me and gives a little nod. She is not, as I feared, consumed with jealousy. I glance at the others, driving my bow, and when I look up she is gone.

There's a hired carriage outside waiting for Therese, but I cannot go with her: I walk off alone with my cello. I need to think. Somehow her appearance tonight worries me more than all the times she has performed in public, when her own playing seems to weave a protection round her. When she plays with Schuppanzigh, people smile at the contrast: she is not then part of the web of gossip surrounding the Count; which reminds me that we are to play Opus 95 again at Maria's tomorrow, though only, I hope, among our friends. The frost bites down to my bones and the stars wheel round the sky as I shuffle towards the Burg. I feel cut off from the world. I walk on to the Stepansdom, and the candles always lit. It is peaceful but much too cold, so I go along to the Schwan and drink schnapps. No, I do not want to see Therese again just yet. I limp to Countess Erdody's house and stay the night.

In the light of morning, the 27th, while even Maria's room is cold, I see her thin neck awry on the pillow like a dead bird. But when she wakes she brims, amazingly, with energy. Today is her, and our, big day. I am sent to make sure that Anna is ready to come and help as soon as may be. Weiss will bring Sophie with him tonight.

It is noon when I come home. The windows are bright but most of the living-room is in shadow. Therese is fondling little Johann on the ottoman while Anna prepares her clothes. The little boy is docile, taking each moment as it comes. Now and then he sings to himself, half-formed fragments of what he has heard. He calls Therese and Anna 'Mutti' without distinction. Leaving Therese to practise, Anna and I take him to Schuppanzigh's wife to be looked after. Mechthilt, of course, adores him. He has the fair curly hair and bright blue eyes of a cherub.

My Anna, with her gentle eyes, is looking sturdy and in her prime. As men light the lamps I look fondly at her white cap, beneath which is tucked up the wonderful mass of her hair. These streets are so familiar to her now, and I think that it would be nice to have a house like Schuppanzigh's, with a shared garden behind it. Why not stay in Vienna? If only, I think, I could be sure that I would be left in peace; or rather that my own restlessness would subside. Then there is the question of Therese, without a husband. People will talk of it, when they have more time on their hands: they might even, mistakenly, connect it with the French Captain. Therefore Breslau is the best plan. When the time is right I will speak to Anna. And yet, I have heard from a merchant that Anna's parents have disappeared. The farm is a ruin, and the old couple are nowhere to be seen.

***

Maria has sent a cabriolet to bring Therese, and I am glad to see that she arrives dressed in black. Weiss and Sophie are here already, along with Schuppanzigh and Hans. Then the main guest, Princess Lichnowsky, arrives on the arm of her protégé, young Mayseder. The fire blazes cheerily, and the blood-red hangings keep out all the cold. Madam Ertmann and the Major are also present, along with Zmeskall, Peter Andreyich and some other old men. When Maria introduces him to Princess Lichnowsky, I recognise Talleyrand. I hear her gasp before she succumbs to the charm of his long mobile face and humorous glinting eyes. Standing behind him is the tall, clean-shaven figure of his amanuensis, the former Captain Ramballe. The Princess leans more heavily on Mayseder's arm. Anna and Sophie bring wine to the guests while we musicians gather in one corner, until the Countess claps and introduces Mayseder and Hans.

The clarinet sonata is an interesting piece. Young Hans is capable, confident and cheery; like a punctilious Pan. Mayseder at the piano strains towards an idea: the piping of the clarinet thrown against a scattered bass. And then something remarkable: a lilting, swaying tune passed from one to the other, making our ears and noses twitch and followed, for dessert, by a rapid jig. I am watching them through the great cheval-glass on the wall, in which I can see half of myself next to half of Schuppanzigh, who now grins and nudges me.

'Our young colleague has learned the art of theft. Did it sound familiar?'

'Somewhat,' I answer, 'Should I know?'

'You of all people should – the ending of J.S. Bach's fourth cello suite!'

When the plates and glasses are full and there is no more to do, Maria seats Anna and Sophie out of the way, next to Monsieur Ramballe. As she flutters round Talleyrand, and Mayseder gallantly kisses Princess Lichnowsky's hand, Hans and Therese, Weiss and Schuppanzigh, share a joke by the fire, their arms around each other like peasants at harvest-time. And so it is I, standing alone, who see Beethoven and Madame Brentano come in; and with them, Count Rasumovsky, who goes first to greet his old father.

Like some huge dark lily, Antonie Brentano fills the room with subtle joy. I hear Madame Ertmann gasp in admiration. But suddenly the Count takes Sophie's hand and leads her out, away, up beyond that Madame Brentano, bending his head in tribute to her hair, her eyes and her short, stumpy but vibrant figure. He and she stand hand in hand before the mirror: he in white and she in black, the tableau of themselves. Then someone, I think Therese, plays a little waltz; he and she take a few steps, and we all applaud. Beethoven shouts 'bravo' in a voice that shakes the room.

Zmeskall, I think to myself, as we rather hurriedly place our chairs, will have many things to report. But thankfully I am whirled into Opus 95. I do not even worry about Therese, in fact I smile at her almost as happily as Weiss; and in the playing tonight I somehow resolve my question about the *Allegretto*.

Talleyrand is playing dice, but they fall quite noiselessly. His long left hand plays his right hand, and his face wills which will win. But he is listening too. Rasumovsky sits by Sophie and listens with an open smile. The Princess stares and stares, and her mouth drops open as Therese's violin leaps like a trout from a stream. During the stunned applause Rasumovsky quietly shakes Beethoven's hand. Soon, however, he makes his excuses. His long dark face is hollow with exhaustion. He nods to Peter Andreyich, who shuffles up to Countess Erdody and politely takes his leave.

'Ah,' cries the Princess, 'I am tired Andrei, after that. Take me home with you!' She too embraces the little Countess, snuffling down into her hair. Josef Mayseder looks askance, then smiles and shrugs. Sophie leaps to her feet, eyes blazing at the Princess, but I see that Ramballe has caught her hand and is speaking quietly into her ear until, with a struggle, she lets her passion subside. Five minutes later Zmeskall also departs, but he cannot refrain from mentioning Count Rasumovsky's own mysterious composition, also a string quartet; he wonders if the Comte de Talleyrand has heard of it?

'Like everyone else,' says the French ambassador. 'But, my dear sir, it has come at an unfortunate time. Vienna today quite clearly has all the music it needs.' And so, with a few words that Zmeskall will now feel obliged to repeat, that subject of mockery sinks into oblivion. The only guests remaining are Talleyrand and Ramballe.

'Well,' Beethoven exclaims, in his barbaric French, 'and what do you really think of the Russians, Monsieur Comte? Russia! I nearly went there once… I suppose that you have been to St Petersburg?' Talleyrand answers gravely that he has not had that pleasure.

'Ah, then you are like us –you half-understand them, no?'

'Indeed,' smiles Talleyrand, 'it is like your music. I see patterns, nothing more.'

'But Count Rasumovsky,' says Ramballe, in a dry, papery voice that makes me wonder if it can be the same man, 'is a man of taste and heart. His instincts are for peace and equality.' Once more he has Sophie by the hand. We have drawn ourselves haphazardly towards the fire. Maria sits with her little head sideways against the back of a chair, with one eye open. Her soirée, so far, has gone well.

'A man, indeed,' says Talleyrand, almost to himself, 'but he is not Russia.'

Beethoven has not heard. 'The Count, of course,' he declares, 'is hardly Russian. Neither is he Austrian. He seems part English, part French.'

'I think,' says Madame Brentano's quiet voice, 'the Count will never quite know who he is. Somehow it slips from his grasp.'

We pause. It has the ring of truth. I look at Sophie and see a crooked, defeated smile. Yet tonight the Count has publicly acknowledged her, confirming the rumours and defying opinion. And we all applauded. Such a thing might reach the ears of the Tsar himself.

'Tells us how,' exclaims Maria, 'one can save one's country? How can anyone save Poland, or Hungary?'

'One tries to make one's aims accord with the other's conscience. If that is not possible, one simply does what one can.'

When Prussia and Russia marched into Paris last year and planned to destroy the bridges over the Seine, Talleyrand renamed one bridge the 'Kaiser' and the other one the 'Tsar'. The bridges were left alone.

With a sly look Maria remarks that Princess Lichnowsky seems calmer and happier than she has ever been; at which Mayseder, who has been sitting in the corner vacated by Peter Andreyich, gets up and awkwardly takes his leave. The fire has sunk to its embers. Sophie looks tired and tearful. When Madame Brentano offers to take her and Weiss back to the palace she merely nods. Captain Ramballe has sat among us like a statue, but as we all rise to depart he suddenly kneels down before Sophie as if he would kiss her feet and she, smiling gently, touches him on the head.

Under a shower of blessings from Maria, Hans, Schuppanzigh, Beethoven in his crumpled hat, Anna, Therese and I step out into the street, all so warmed to the marrow that we can laugh at the frost. It is another beautiful, cold black starry night. Hans leads us off, tootling on his clarinet. First he apes Mayseder's tune, then he mocks the peasant dance from the Sixth, doubling the tempo and running out of wind. We roll like a comet through the frozen dark. Hans is for the Schwan, with Beethoven and Schuppanzigh.

'And Therese!' he commands.

'No, my dear,' says Schuppanzigh.

'Why?' laughs Hans, 'why why why?' And Beethoven joins in.

'If she was a boy,' he says, pouting, with his arm around her waist. She laughs with her eyes and whacks him with her fiddle case. 'Ah, Leonore!' shouts Beethoven. In a moment his greatcoat is thrown on top of her shawl and his hat is on her head. He stands there in his shirt: 'She'll do! We'll keep her in the dark!' And, like a band of grinning cats, they disappear.

'Let her enjoy herself,' says Anna, taking my arm, 'who knows what tomorrow will bring.'

We are walking as briskly as we can, considering my limp and the patches of ice. When we arrive at Schuppanzigh's house we apologise for our lateness.

'You're welcome!' smiles Mechthilt, kissing the sleeping child cradled in her brawny arms, 'I would keep him longer! And where's that husband of mine? Off with his young man, I suppose.'

'Have you met him?' I ask, intrigued. It suddenly occurs to me that Schuppanzigh and Hans are inseparable. Once or twice I have played the '*Archduke*' with Ignaz and Madame Ertmann. Hans is always there.

'Oh, of course, I've nothing against him. Little Hans. He's just a boy. Mind you, his mother should take more care of him. I've put him in the bath right here! *And* she should stop acting the Countess, eh? In the end those people spit on us for fun. People are saying the Count will marry Lichnowsky's widow, and become an Austrian. In Madame Sophie's place I'd get away from that palace and let what must be, be.'

The cold wakes little Johann up. He rests on Anna's hip and smiles at me from under his shawl, making little squeaks like a bat as together we carefully walk the narrow streets of peaceful sleepers. The smells of dampened fires perfume the chilly air.

***

It is afternoon before I collect my cello from Maria's. Yet again I heft it through the streets towards the palace. As I had hoped, the orchard door is open. Workmen are attaching a flue which runs across from the storeroom to the new extension, while Karl and Peter Andreyich look on. I pass them quickly and walk on between the iron trees, in order to see my friend from Breslau, Weiss. I am still *not* entirely sure about the *Allegretto*. There is also a difficult moment in the *Larghetto*. I want to play it through with Weiss, at the point where his response enters over mine.

I can scc a candlc lit inside the cottage. Frost is beginning to harden back on the grass. I go up the little path, push the door ajar, and find myself in front of the Count and Sophie. He is drinking rum. I smell it on the air, not much warmer than outside. I see a bald patch on his crown. His body, as I have never seen it, sags inside the stiff white uniform. Sophie's eyes have still their gleam, but her face is round and soft and her hand is linked in his. Where Weiss is they do not know. As I retreat the Count, with even more than his customary politeness, bestirs himself to say that this new quartet, the Opus 95, is really and truly the strangest and the most wonderful yet.

Returning through the long, cold ballroom, past the library, I find Josef Mayseder wrapping himself to go out. He looks pleased to see me again and walks down into the street beside me, not offering to carry my cello, but slowing his pace to mine by looking about into the shadows. Our ways are the same, he says, towards his father's house. In the windows of the Graben the lamps are being lit. In a palace courtyard grooms are putting in the horses. There is no-one out but ourselves and a few creeping beggars. It is dark and cold. By the statue of the Plague, in between the bubbling fountains, Mayseder stops dead and turns to face me, looking around as he does to make sure no-one can hear: 'You must be careful. *Please* be careful. Be discreet.'

'What are you talking about?'

'They are all against the Count: Metternich, his own people. They are against Beethoven's music, especially his quartets. They are against Countess Erdody.' I turn and carry on towards home. He continues to walk beside me. 'So what,' I say, 'am I to do? I have to play at the Count's ball, and so do you.'

'Indeed. That is unfortunate. But otherwise, you know – you could avoid playing Beethoven. We could avoid being linked to Rasumovsky. Do you remember what Rothschild said? In future, you see, we need to be more Austrian.'

Of course he is talking about Therese as well as me. Well, she will retire, soon. But it is too late, I think, to change my allegiances; to seek employment with a Lobkowitz or Kinsky, or to dance attendance on Princess Lichnowsky's friends. I will not give up my friendship with Maria, whether or not I become her tutor. I will not pretend to care nothing for the Count, or for Sophie, or Weiss. It is not as easy as he thinks to dismiss the past.

We have reached my door. I am perturbed, and angry. I look at him, with his light, soft hair and his immaculate dress. Even when he is dressed in the Count's red livery he looks well. I have an urge to strike him – this youth whose music is nothing, who is afraid of his own shadow. But of course he may be right about Rasumovsky; and when great ones fall those beneath them suffer. 'Very well,' I say, 'come upstairs with me.' It is time I gave him something else to think about. Anna is dozing with the boy on her lap, but when she sees Mayseder her face lights up.

'See here, Josef,' she calls, 'your son!'

To hell, I think, with her and everything. How could she be so simple, as to put her faith in this dandy? Mayseder is already looking round to escape, but I forestall him. I feel a pang at Anna's expression when she sees my intention, but all the same I turn around without a word, and, taking my cello with me, begin the long walk to Maria Erdody's house.

11. Weiss (29 December)

This one night in Anna's arms feels as natural as frost on the window-panes. I seem to float above us both, seeing myself snug and warm. Yes, it all seems natural, even though Therese, who came back in the early hours, sleeps next door by the embers of the fire, on the rug with her little boy curled up at her side. When we rise at the first shimmy of winter light we are like potatoes newly lifted and shining. And then Anna tells me that she and Sophie are sisters. Today, at her birthday party, Sophie will acknowledge her, but Anna just had to tell somebody first. Their mother came from Poland, but Sophie was not a Polish orphan: she ran away from their father, who beat them. She ran away from the farm. Now, Anna says, their parents have disappeared, and she has heard the farm is a ruin. Neither of the old people can read or write, and to search for them would be impossible. She and Linke, and Sophie, can only wait and hope.

As I walk briskly away, almost floating, I think, yet again, of the night in Breslau years ago, of Anna and I and Sophie then, and of Anna's little girl, Therese, and of my passion for Anna; and I did not know they were sisters! My passion was a passing craze, or would have been, I suppose; it burned up again last night, but we shall do nothing more. It was one night, one memory that I can have to myself. I won't let it trouble me. It was Linke whom I was looking for, after I learned that he was looking for me. Hans and I came home together from Schuppanzigh, who had been coaching Therese for a soirée in the Palais – Duchess Wilhemine de Sagan. So we three walked back together, leaving Therese at Anna's to dress. Sophie was in the cottage alone. I smelt liquor on her breath. The fire wasn't lit but I soon had it going, and suddenly she smiled, and began to lay out food on the table – bread, cold ham, some veal and cheese. There was a bottle of wine. We had had soup at Schuppanzigh's, but we didn't mind some more. Once we had eaten, she straightened herself to go to the palace, and it was then that she mentioned Linke's visit, with his cello, by which I knew he had come about a quartet, either the one we played last night or the one we must play tomorrow.

'I miss him, you know,' Sophie added, meaning Beethoven.

'You saw him last night,' I smiled

'I know I did, and I don't dislike your precious Madame Brentano. It's just not the same as the old days.'

She left us at eight o'clock, slipping in her shawl across the frozen grass to the ballroom, with its fine new doors. I watched her and thought of all the many times she had left like that. Then I thought of how I had crossed that space, before this extension was built, and how I had waited there with Fritz to play the second quartet, and how I had kissed her; how it had been a flash in my dull life, like the time on the river-bank. Hans drained the rest of his wine. 'Are you going out?' he asked.

'Well I might. And you?'

'Ignaz said I could come to that Duchess if I wished; in the hotel near the Burg.'

'Very well,' I said, 'I'll walk with you. I must really go and see Linke – two old men together!'

I damped the fire, pulled out the wood, but left in the few embers of coal. Then we walked off at a hot pace and went our own ways rapidly. Hans is becoming a good violist, and in the orchestra he is second clarinet. Mayseder chose him to play that piece at the Countess Erdody's, and as far as I could judge he played it well. I thought that very likely tonight Hans would play duets with 'Leonore' at the Duchess de Sagan's: Ignaz would arrange it so. Then I went on to Linke's and found Anna alone with the child.

It is mid-day already, so long since I came back home, almost time to leave again, and I am wondering where she can be. Where *I* have been is still at the back of my mind. It was one of those things. Prowling in the orchard, I have looked up through the bare trees and seen the lights in the Count's study. He has been at work for hours. At last she arrives, smiling, and goes upstairs to change. I am expecting finery – a green silk dress to match her eyes – but she appears in a plain, clean smock, just like Anna wears. But where has she been? I am unused to asking her questions, but today I'm impatient.

She smiles at me: 'Can you not guess?'

'I thought you must be with the Count.'

'I left him sleeping long ago. I went straight out.'

'Yes, but where?'

'Oh Franz, can you not guess?'

Suddenly I guess: 'Beethoven! And how was he?' I ask.

She thinks a moment, looking inwards, then comes out with one word: 'Bursting!' I see him, as in the old days, when he was such a friend, and I see us drifting away, not knowing what work he is doing, or who his friends and enemies are.

'Madame Brentano,' says Sophie sadly, 'does not give him inspiration. Perhaps she is just too beautiful in herself.'

'And you,' I say, 'did you help him?' Sometimes Beethoven would claim that Sophie had been his muse, and it was hard to say whether he was joking or not.

'Those days are gone,' she says, 'only look at me!'

Once more we walk across the orchard, past the long pipe coming out of the wall, over to the little door, and out into the street. It is an afternoon of low cloud and dank chill, almost threatening rain. The Count, if he has time to observe, will be hoping that tomorrow is fine and frosty, everything looking its best for his great ball.

I think about this afternoon's party and wonder if the Count also has plans to celebrate Sophie's name-day. As we come round the corner to the front of the palace I see Mayseder, who has declined the Countess's invitation to our party, hurrying towards the entrance, as if he were late for an appointment. Sophie is looking the other way. Now she takes me by the arm and says: 'You have not noticed then?' I look at her. She seems quite calm. 'I am pregnant, Franz, and it is yours.'

This summer I thought perhaps it might happen, when the Count was away in France, and it was like our early days in Breslau, except that Hans, so tall and handsome, would come and go with his viola, while Sophie and I were happy to let the warm days slide past. We sat out at the back of the cottage, facing away from the palace, down towards the canal and the Birkenstock house, and Sophie would rub her bare feet against the grass. But she did not get pregnant then; it has happened now. I look into her face in astonishment. Her mind has been so much upon the palace, the Count and the Princess, she has been so worried for him, that I had forgotten that we made love, too, not so very long ago: but it is true, we did.

'I know it isn't his,' she says. 'It will be ours – after so long.'

'Sophie,' I say suddenly, 'couldn't we leave all this and go back to Breslau, and start again?' It seems to me I might escape, from everything. She shakes her head.

'The Count needs me. And I will fight for him, as I would fight for you again. You have no idea what they try to do to him. It would play on anyone's mind. They have him married off already! They mock him with his quartet, and with me. Then he has somehow to have his horrible father meet the Tsar in private. The old man troubles him. Princess Lichnowsky drives him mad.'

We turn into the Krugerstrasse where Countess Erdody's windows are lighted and shining down into the gloomy street. I take Sophie's arm. I am afraid for her, for the child. Things could go wrong, like last time. And I ask myself again, why must she love the Count?

'Do you remember,' she says, 'how the Archduke and the Emperor himself used to smile at me? But now I must be shut away!'

Inside, Sophie is claimed by the little Countess. They go off and whisper together. This morning Anna had said to me that Sophie's reason for announcing their sisterhood was that she was tired of having to pretend. Perhaps, I think, with Therese now famous as well as us, the Count's quartet, she somehow wants to defy the gossips. 'All the same,' Anna had added, 'I am worried about her.'

Schuppanzigh sits heavily on one of the red, upholstered chairs. He looks rather wearily at Therese, who has appropriated the Countess's red chaise longue and rests her feet in Hans's lap. Anna is standing between Linke and

147

myself. Glancing sideways I see their hands – hers smooth and light, his long and gnarled – move as if to touch, and then drop back to their sides. The meat pies and strudels, and the champagne, are waiting, but it seems as if someone else is expected. Countess Erdody looks up at the clock, then, chasing off Therese and Hans, she seats herself and beckons Anna and Sophie to take their places beside her. Looking carefully, smilingly at us all she makes the announcement on their behalf: Sophie and Anna are sisters! I find myself as open-mouthed as if I had no idea, indeed it seems as if I had somehow forgotten, while on the others' faces I see various types of puzzlement. Hans and Therese look at each other. After a moment they grin, and he punches her shoulder, as if to say that it makes no difference, he will make fun of her let their parents say what they please. Linke looks from one to the other, and then at the little Countess, trying to adjust his ideas. Finally he looks at me, and something in my blank expression makes him smile. And now Schuppanzigh, who has been looking at each of us in turn, puts back his head and roars with laughter; and suddenly we all join in.

'So,' says the little Countess, 'we are all happy together! It only remains for you, young lady, to kiss your aunt.' Therese goes forward dutifully but rocking slightly, as I remember she did when she was disguised as a boy. How strange, I think, that everyone, Sophie included, came to think that she *was* a boy, even though they knew she was not. And then did Sophie ever manage to take her to meet with Anna in those years, or even bring Anna to her? Perhaps the former if, perhaps, she could think of her as a girl, as her niece in fact, when they were outside the palace – but I cannot guess.

It is whilst we are eating and raising our glasses to Sophie's name-day that Captain Ramballe appears. I can tell from her look that she has been expecting him. I think I recognise him solely by those dark eyes, even though they are like coals which have now burned themselves out. I suppose there is also the upright bearing, and the way in which (although I do not think he did it before, in the street, so long ago) he kisses Sophie's hand. I go back to an old puzzle. Why did this

Frenchman abduct Therese? Why did he arrange, if he did, to give her back to Sophie? But it didn't work: it was I who found her on the riverbank.

Therese is standing by me now, jigging, as always, with her own thoughts, although she is now my height and her figure is fully developed. I gently jog her bowing arm, and she turns and smiles reminiscently. She has become a marvel, but I almost regret that she no longer needs anyone's help. I wonder, though, what she will do when the Congress finally ends, if it ever ends. I ask her now what she played last night at the Duchess de Sagan's, thinking as I do, that I should like to have been there. I should like to play more myself, apart from in the orchestra. I should like to see these great ones in their homes.

'I played a Bach sonata,' she says. 'Ignaz thought they would like it, but they didn't.'

She is dressed in black again today. She looks tired now. Her life is no more natural than when she lived in the palace. But this is where we are.

The others are talking quietly in groups, just as in other salons before the tea is served: Linke with Ramballe and Countess Erdody; Schuppanzigh with Sophie and Anna, who looks at Therese and myself, and divides a smile between us. I am expecting the little Countess to move us about, but it is Sophie who claps her hands and beckons us all into a circle. Then she turns to her sister.

'I did wrong,' she says, 'to send the Captain to you. I ask your pardon, Anna. Of course I only meant to surprise you; I did not think of what would happen.'

'Ah, Madame,' cries Ramballe, 'all the fault, the shame, is mine! You could not help your spirits – and you must keep them now.'

Once more this strange fellow throws himself at Sophie's feet. Once more Sophie ruffles his hair. All of us have fallen silent – Hans, Schuppanzigh, Linke – with serious faces. I am still expecting the Countess to somehow take command, when Therese leans forward, pats Ramballe on the shoulder, and says to him, brightly: 'Oh, you know, we don't mind!

In no time at all we arc like one family, as if our celebrations beforehand had been some kind of pretence; we eat and drink with pleasure, and Schuppanzigh makes jokes so terrible as to be worthy of Beethoven himself. Only Linke, apart from the Captain, still looks rather serious. I try to avoid Anna, but when we do exchange a glance she looks quite calm. I look at her hair, darker than Sophie's, falling halfway down her back, as she turns around, and I sense that she is longing just to go home.

Countess Erdody, who also seems much taken with the Captain, asks him how he came to be so late. With grave apologies he explains that he was detained on his way at the Rasumovsky palace, where he had to deliver invitations from M. Talleyrand, for Prince Rasumovsky and Princess Lichnowsky.

'I was asked to wait,' he says, 'but after waiting some time I was told that neither of them could be found.' From a distance I feel Sophie, who still occupies the chaise, give a sudden start.

'You mean,' she calls, 'that they were not at home to you?'

'They could not be found,' he repeats. Something strikes him, for he goes across to her, and sits looking at her as if he would kneel again.

Ignaz and Hans – one bulky, one slender – walk ahead of us on our return. It has begun to freeze. Sophie has my arm. From time to time her thoughts bring her up with a jerk, after which her pace quickens almost to a run. She will have no peace now from her jealousy of the Princess until she has seen the Count; until, I suppose, he has taken her in his arms. I think again of how we sat together last summer, when the Count was away for months, facing away from the cottage, the apples above us ripe and her bare feet trailing into the grass. If she had fallen pregnant then she might now be as round-bellied as she was with Hans. We might have had to go – away from the Count, the Congress; it would have been better so. There is, as yet, no sign of the child, and I wonder if I am the only one to know. I think probably not. I wonder why I could not throw myself, like Ramballe, at Sophie's feet; for I love her in spite of everything.

Ignaz turns around to tell us that he and Hans are going upstairs to look over a score. I would prefer to use our side-entrance, but Sophie tugs me forward up the steps, and now the new young porter who has replaced old Franz suddenly appears with a coat across his arm. The Count has left instructions for Madame Sophie to go up to his study and sew on some silver buttons which are waiting there. The coat is for Peter Andreyich. Sophie holds it up as if it were a crow.

'And where is the Count?' The porter does not know. 'I will bring it to him, wherever he is.' Sophie limps up the stairs.

I make my way past the library, through the ballroom and its wooden extension, to the cottage. I open my door and find a man sitting alone in the dark. I know him by his silhouette: it is the Count. He sees me and, at the second attempt, gets a spark from his flint to the candle. There is a hint of warmth from the embers of yesterday's fire. They bring coal in wagons from Breslau, but it is not enough. In the kitchens they are burning sawdust.

'Has she gone to sew those buttons? And – how is she – happy?' He speaks in German, to which he gives a strange, rippling effect. I cannot remember when he last spoke to me, if he ever did. I am lost for words. 'Sit down,' he says.

This has never been my cottage. Everything belongs to him except my table, my cups and my own viola. Yet he is so haggard, as white as his uniform, that I almost pity him. Suddenly he lays his hand on the table near to mine: a hand with supple, tapering digits, almost longer than Linke's, and speaks: 'This is why I am here. You do not love her, but she will not leave you. She cannot let go, by herself. If I make you rich enough to live as you like, will you divorce her?'

What, I think, should I do with money? I have never thought of it. I can't imagine what I should do. How could he think that things could suddenly be so different, when I walked her home just now?

'If,' I say, 'she doesn't want me, I will give her up to you.'

'Come,' he says, 'I will soon retire from public life. Her new child will have a good home. You will be free, and I will always care for her.'

I can suddenly imagine it – this divorce. I would have a proper home, like Schuppanzigh. Hans might live with me. We should make music with our friends. Therese might come and visit - with Anna, or Linke, or both. But there would be no Sophie.

'But if she needs me,' I say, 'I cannot do it.'

'Need you, Herr Musician? Go and find her and tell her that I will give up all for her! Tell her it is time! Go and find her. Go!'

The ground outside is hard as iron. I retrace my steps. Last night I slept with Anna. It will not happen again. I want to be with Sophie now, to be with her as often before; to ease her fears; to put my arm around her. I can ease her jealousy, and tell her the Count loves her; but this time I will tell her that I love her too. I climb slowly up the great, wide, red staircase. In all this time I have never been to the first floor: I do not know where the Count's study is. On the landing I meet Schuppanzigh, coming down.

'I heard a noise outside,' he says. 'Did you see Hans? He was on his way to you.' I shake my head: 'Did you see Sophie?'

As we look down to the hallway Princess Lichnowsky appears. She pauses below a moment, then rushes up towards us like a wounded animal. She is wearing red slippers and the red robe with golden dragons, and there are tears in her eyes. A moment later Mayseder passes through the hall with his fiddle under his arm, and goes out quickly through the front door. Finally, the servant Karl comes out from the Canova room with a duster in his hand, and stands looking into space.

Schuppanzigh pulls on his hat. He urges me to go to the cottage and see if Hans and Sophie are there. He is quite sure, he says, that Sophie is not up here. The orchard key is in my pocket. I go back down with Ignaz, past the ominous figure of Karl, walk round into the Donaustrasse and through the little door in the wall. I turn and lock it again behind me. I notice a great moon overhead. As I approach the cottage I see Hans standing in our garden, near the little mound where our dead child is buried.

'Did you see the window?' he asks me. I shake my head. He looks at me with a kind of furious despair. 'Come inside,' he says. The candle is still burning. We sit down at the table. Hans begins to speak: 'I was coming out of the palace when I saw the Count out here, and just then I heard a crash and mother shouting, over there. Then we both ran and mother was there with a stone in her hand, but the window was broken already, and inside the room I saw…' he pauses and shudders, 'Herr Mayseder and the Princess. Then the Count took mother away.'

He brings his fingers up to his face, as if he neither wants to see nor to be seen. Then he brings them down with a jerk. 'You can't help her,' he says.

12. Schuppanzigh (30-31 December)

In my nightmares Hans is raped and tortured in St Petersburg. Sometimes it's a fair-haired prince who has the whole skin of a bear tied upon his naked body, and uses the claws in obscene ways. Other times a group of Cossacks beat him with their gleaming sabres. His perfect skin is rent and trickles blood. In these dreams Hans writhes as if he likes their brutality; then he begins to scream, and I wake up. This only makes me gentler and more careful of him by day. He is petulant and confused; gracious sometimes, and admiring; troubled, with a hint of spite; which made it sweeter when we returned from his mother's birthday party and fell into each other's arms. Love was in the air yesterday, engulfing us all: my love mingled in with what I sensed in others, even in Linke's woman, Anna, and the strange Frenchman Ramballe - people I hardly know. Yes, and then: to touch and be touched; to feel his perfect skin, and the soft, red flame of his head; and to make him spurt.

Afterwards, though, he wanted to be off. Part of me wanted to keep him longer, part to be alone and reflect. I could just glimpse him from up here, as he went across from the palace to the cottage. Wearing only my shirt I boldly flung open the window, embracing the freezing air; and then I heard the sound of breaking glass, followed by poor Sophie's voice. I leant a little further out, but everything was dark.

Early next morning I am at home with Mechthilt, when Hans comes to tell me exactly what Sophie has done; but I have it already from Madame De Sagan's footman, who has it from the Duchess's maid, who has a relation in the Rasumovsky palace. Scandal is in the air. Hans says that neither he nor his father slept, although they went to bed, because of the cold. Weiss, tormented and helpless, went out early to wander the streets. There is no reason, Hans says with sorrow, why he should blame himself. This is how his mother is. But everyone is looking at them: he heard some servants laughing this morning as he passed by; and tonight is the great ball, and he is afraid to play in the orchestra. People will be pointing at him, as well as at Mayseder; and what will the Princess do? He remembers her temper from when he was at Gratz.

We must have courage, I tell him. Besides, most of the people tonight will only have eyes for the Tsar. And we know that the Count will not do Sophie any harm –it may be for the best that he keeps her out of the way. And afterwards, if he wants to, Hans can stay with us until it all dies down; and so, of course, can Weiss. It will be like old times.

Mechthilt plies him with food and ruffles his hair. We live now in a little house with an apple-tree at the back, and we have a five-plate stove whose panels are wrought with violins where she makes broth and cakes. It keeps in the flames, it cannot cause fire, but it keeps us warm; when it gets too hot Mechthilt likes to stand in the open door, or even right out in the street, in the falling snow, in her chemise. Our neighbours are used to her and equably return her greetings.

She is standing out there this morning, airing the kitchen, and Hans is eating his eggs, when Beethoven arrives. Soon he's eating eggs too, while he talks to me:

'Madame Brentano wants to hear the violin sonatas. It must be tomorrow. You and I will play them – '

'What, all of them?'

He looks up and grins like a schoolboy. 'I forgot you are old and fat. Which do you suggest?'

'Number six, I think, and number ten. After Opus Ninety-Five you should show your peaceful side.'

He considers. 'Yes, you old fraud, it would be best. It will be better for her to *imagine* that I can be at peace, even if she knows it's not true. It is a parting gift, Ignaz. She and Franz are leaving for Dresden.'

'Until the Spring?' I ask. He shakes his head. 'No, forever: Franz Brentano is a good man; I can no longer come between them, no matter how I feel, and - Antonie agrees.'

He covers his face and lets out a sob, while Hans looks at him open-mouthed. I look away towards the stove, which Mechthilt has just opened to throw in a little wood. I look at the spurt of yellow flame before she closes it again, and in that moment I realise that I must renounce my Hans. Sooner or later he is bound to leave me; though he no longer minds the discipline, the hours of practice, there are times, more often lately, when I can tell he would much rather be somewhere else, if he had somewhere to go. I shall propose a separation, and find him another teacher: then, after a little while, we shall be like old friends.

'I am sorry to intrude,' says a dry voice behind me. Like some ghost from the past a French cavalry officer, dressed as if for battle, stands outside the door. I beckon Ramballe to enter, loudly assuring Beethoven that I know the gentleman, who comes in cautiously, bowing to each of us, and to Hans not least. We cannot help but be astonished at this upright figure in the green dolman and breeches, red epaulettes, collar and cuffs, and with the fur pelisse on his shoulder; like a ghost indeed, because the great moustache of 1809 is absent from his face.

'I do hope,' he says to me, 'all will be well with Madame Sophie.'

'Madame Sophie!' shouts Beethoven. 'What want *you* with Sophie?'

'Why, sir, she is my friend. I want her never to be unhappy. We must hope that the Count –'

'Count be damned - and Frenchmen too!'

'As I said,' says Ramballe loudly, 'I am a true friend to Madame. I am also proud to be French!'

Mechthilt grabs her bowls and slams them down on the table. Then she lifts her pot from the stove, plonks down the sweet-smelling broth and, hand on hip, waves her ladle right in our faces. The Frenchman smiles and bows as he accepts his ladleful, while opposite him Beethoven looks up from under puzzled brows.

'Why, all of a sudden,' I ask, 'are you in uniform? Do you intend to wear it tonight, at the ball?'

'Indeed,' Ramballe replies, looking at me wearily, 'I wear it because the Tsar is bringing his personal guard. You may call it, if you will, a gesture of defiance, or a reminder that France has not ceased to exist. It would be better, of course, to leave these things to the politicians. The Tsar does not need his guard inside the Rasumovsky palace! But some of his people are ready to threaten war. So they use his guard to frighten the rest of us, and we have to show that we will not be cowed.'

His words remind me that I must soon be off to the palace. I will persuade Hans to stay here and rest in our bed; perhaps I will have time to watch him fall asleep.

'And what can I do for you?' Remembering that Talleyrand has sent out some invitations, I presume that, at last, he too wants a little music; hence, the Frenchman has come to hire me.

'I hardly know why I have come.' Ramballe lifts his dark eyes and turns them full on Hans, who looks at me as if for help. 'You are, if I have understood, all associated with Prince Rasumovsky. Therefore when he falls from grace it may affect you too. He is sure to be replaced as head of the Russian delegation.'

'I have heard that too,' I say, 'but he will still be the wealthiest man in Vienna.' Ramballe looks down, as if he knew something more. But, unless the Count has committed treason, I cannot think how he should cease to be the Count. I don't believe that he will marry Princess Lichnowsky, but he will stay in Vienna just the same.

'I have heard,' says Beethoven, 'that Rasumovsky gives you French a hard time in the Congress, but I suppose you deserve it.'

'Our positions regarding France's border can be resolved. The little German electors, too, will give up their absolute rights, providing the concession towards the Jews is dropped. The problem we face is Russia's claim to Poland. There Rasumovsky is under pressure. The Tsar's people think that he is too close to Metternich, which is why they want him replaced. They say he has lived here too long. But still, the other powers will never let Poland be swallowed up by Russia.'

'And what do you think of what has happened in France?'

Ramballe leans back and lets out a sigh. 'That is hard to

express. My family werc royalists, from the west of France. In my twenties I had to hide from the terror. But those of us who served the Emperor will never forget. We led the soldier's life, but we knew we were also serving France. Now the royalists who have come back want to tear down everything, even the Arc de Triomphe.'

'You are my age! And you fought-'

'At Rivoli, Ulm, Austerlitz, Jena, Eylau, Friedland and Wagram.'

'And Moscow?'

Ramballe inclines his head. Beethoven looks at him with an open smile. I remember now that Ramballe heard and admired 'Leonore', as it was then called – almost ten years ago. I wonder if Beethoven even remembers that time. I wonder if Ramballe has been to hear *Fidelio*.

'And what will *you* do after this Congress? Will you stay here? Will you marry?'

Ramballe shakes his head.

'Come!' says Beethoven, holding out his hand, 'we shall be friends, you and I.'

'I am honoured,' says Ramballe, taking it, 'but I cannot tell you my plans, for I have none at all. I was in the Russian campaign,' he says quietly. 'My servant saved my life, but he died. The frost went into me. It went through me. I shall never recover, and perhaps I deserve it; but I am honoured, sir.'

***

Not too sweet,' says the Count, 'I want them to hear…' He does not finish, but of course I understand. He is tired. His hair, which was still black two years ago, is tinged with grey. Now he wants them to hear what it is – Opus 59, the third. He seems to expand in his armchair, like a bear emerging from slumber. Then he smiles and says: 'It will go well, will it not? Your last performance! Well, nothing lasts for ever. You, and I, deserve a little peace.'

He leaves me there in the library. I have nothing to do now but wait for the others to come in for our last rehearsal. It is as warm as in my own house. I look at the orange flames from the logs, the spurts of pallid yellow and blue from some lumps of coal. There is a knock at the door, and the French maid, Natalie, comes in with our scores, which are kept in the Count's study. It is a long time since we all went down into the kitchens at night; those times when, after playing in secret to Sophie, the Count and Peter Andreyich, we could relax with the maids. Now even Natalie has shadows under her eyes. Her whole body sags a little and the impish look has gone, leaving her like a sick kitten. I get up to help her, ensuring that each of the scores is on the right stand; opening my own and glancing, for the hundredth time, at the bold strokes of Beethoven's pen. This, of course, is normally Sophie's task, and – divining that she knows – I ask Natalie how she is. Natalie frowns, and then looks at me anxiously. Of course, she is aware that every gossip in Vienna would like to know where Sophie is right now.

'She is well,' she answers. 'The Count has been so anxious for her! So have I!'

'What about Herr Weiss?' I ask. 'He is anxious too.'

'He has had a message from her. Do not concern yourself.'

I am so grateful to hear this, and yet sad, that I am moved to squeeze her little hand. I will try to send a message back to Hans.

Behind her the door swings open and Peter Andreyich marches in, followed, to my relief, by Weiss, Linke, Mayseder. The old man's skull and twisted ears emerge from a brand-new coat with silver buttons. As they come in I catch a glimpse of Karl in the corridor.

Opus 59, the third: after the clashing moods of the first, the questing of the second, this one, from dissonance to fugue, a balancing unbalance, is a quartet that I will never fully understand. Perhaps it stands apart, as it stands in the middle, between its predecessors and the elegance of the Harp, the love-song of the Serioso. But after all our little dramas it is good to play first fiddle again, to puzzle at the music with some measure of control. We reach the mill-race of the fugue, arrest it, as ever, on that final chord. One play-through has been enough. Our business is only to play it tonight for those with ears to hear, and until then we should get what rest we can.

Weiss packs up his viola sadly. Linke stumps away looking morose and tired. Mayseder, poor boy, scutters off, looking left and right, but not where he is going. Peter Andreyich, our eternal auditor, has also stumped away, and I think that for once we barely noticed his presence, although I am sure he watched us as closely as he always has. I put my hand on Weiss's arm. I tell him Hans is with Mechthilt and ask him how he is himself. He looks at me with surprising calm.

'I have been to the Stepansdom, Ignaz. Sophie asked me to say a prayer. It was strange, you know – not being a catholic. Everything in this city is hard and strange! But I have done it, and now I shall wait. It gave me an idea, too. When I see her again, I will confess to everything. We must have no more secrets.' Strange fellow! I think, and yet I almost envy him. He goes off to that little cottage where, of course, he will practice again, to pass the time. I hang back to gather my thoughts, feeling a moment's content at the smell of warm leather, and the sunlight still slanting faintly into one corner, as if to promise me that some hope will always remain. A damp log hisses loudly in the fire. As I pick up my fiddle to go, the door opens once again.

'Ah - you! I'm glad it's you!' Princess Lichnowsky closes the door behind her. She is still dressed in black. She also has her head covered with a shawl, which she now folds back as she smiles an almost tender smile.

'You can help me,' she says, encouragingly, as if to a small, fat child. I wait, as so often before, for her to collect her thoughts. Even in the early 'musical' days, when she and the old Prince would spend eight months a year in Vienna, both of them would stare into space, at a loss for words, until Beethoven, impatient, would rush to the keyboard and improvise, and they would both nod and smile and conversation would cease to matter.

'I have just,' she announces now, as if she wants the palace to hear, 'been to see Prince Metternich. I asked him to show good-will towards my brother-in-law, who has lived among us so long. And the Prince assured me that he bears the Count no personal grudge. His only duties, he said, were first to defend Austria's interest, and second, to maintain the respect due to all persons of rank.' I place my hands across my stomach, as if to make a bow. I can see that the Princess understands Metternich's meaning. Because of Sophie, of 'Leonore' - even, perhaps, because of Beethoven, the Count is *already* in disgrace. He has acted too freely, just when freedom must give way to order, and the Princess knows there is nothing more she can do. But she will keep her own good name, the name of an ancient family: the gossip about Mayseder will quickly die away.

'I shall *not*,' she says, 'be present at the ball tonight. I intend to leave Vienna, but I must see Madame Weiss, and you must help me to find her. I wish to make my peace.'

The memory comes to me of a woman's cry, which at first I thought was a cry of distress. Then, long ago it was, I did not hesitate. So, once again, I force myself up the spiral stairs, and the Princess follows. The door is not locked – it opens as it did before, and there is Sophie seated on the bed. The room is dim and grey and cold, with a few bare forks of trees far off outside the round windows. The Princess pauses and takes in the tapestries, the rugs and the bed. Sophie, still dressed as when I last saw her, looks down, showing the fold in her chin, and does not move.

'My dear,' says the Princess, 'I am going away. So forgive me, please. Since you love Andrei, I must wish you well.'

Moved by her own words she pulls back her shawl again, throws forward her black mane and stretches her long white fingers out towards Sophie's lap. Sophie looks up as if puzzled. Then, gradually, she widens her eyes that are sea-green in the dimness, and takes the offered hand. Thus they remain for a minute, not looking at each other directly, until Sophie quietly puts her hand back in her lap..'I am so sorry,' she says.

The Princess turns from me to Sophie and back again. There are tears in her eyes.

'Let me take you away,' she says. 'just until tonight is over. Come, we will take my carriage. Am I not right,

Schuppanzigh?'

'You are right, Princess,' I say.

'Where shall we go?'

'To her sister' I say, 'or Countess Erdody; or' – I have a sudden inspiration - 'to Herr Beethoven's apartment. No-one would look for her there.' But Sophie has risen and retreated to the window. I see her glance down at the rug where the trap-door is hidden.

'I must stay here,' she says, 'especially now – now I have seen you Princess. It must have been difficult for you. Ignaz, please go and tell the Count, that I will wait in this room for as long as he likes.'

It might all have been a dream, were it not that daylight is fading from the library. We have just regained it when a servant enters and lights the candles. Princess Lichnowsky goes to the fire and stretches out her hands, and I imagine she is saying farewell to the palace; then I pick up my fiddle once more and follow her out of the room.

There are so many rooms in the palace that I have never seen: the servants' bedrooms of course, or those of the secretaries, and the Princess's suite. Down here, the little room from which comes a tapping noise; the rooms along this corridor occupied by Peter Andreyich; then behind the great front staircase and the Canova room, the entrance to the dining-rooms where tonight the Count will sit down to supper with the Tsar and the Emperor. I go up the stairs.

The windows are clear in the Count's study. The eastern stars are coming out. Secretaries have passed me like a stream dividing; I have waited to be admitted, but I find him alone, looking at the score I once gave him: Opus 95. He looks up, tired and preoccupied, but when I repeat the message he is wreathed in smiles.

'Ah! She loves me! She is mine!'

He leaps up and puts his hand in his pocket, looking, as he does, at the bookshelf in the corner. Can it be, I wonder, that there is one more hidden door? I try to remember the shapes of the trees I have seen, from those windows, and these. I am sure he is grasping a key. Perhaps there is one more door concealed in the corner, hidden behind a tapestry on the other side. How strange for her, to be so near!

Suddenly there are voices, loud, outside, where the messengers stand like statues. Karl bursts in, grim-faced as ever, with the Count's secretary. I slip away, at last, upstairs, and lie down on the bed in my attic, with a blanket against the cold. And so it is two hours more, and the first guests are arriving, when I discover that Natalie is dead.

I have come down in my livery, into the Canova room, where trestles of cold food are laid out for the orchestra. In less than an hour the ball will commence. I have come down to wish Hans luck, and it is he who tells me the news. Weiss seems wholly preoccupied, almost as if, as ever, he is preparing how he intends to play in his mind. Linke looks upset and defiant. Mayseder is trembling and wiping tears away. I wonder if he will manage to lead the orchestra. I too am shocked, but there is no time to think. Around us the other players, who hardly know the palace, eat and drink and talk in murmurs, glancing now and then at us. The young porter found Natalie lying on the cobblestones. It looks as though she must have fallen, perhaps from the Princess's windows. They have put her in one of the stables and washed away the blood.

When the players have left for the ballroom I go up the corner stairs, along the passage and into the hidden balcony. An age ago I sat up here with Sophie. Now as then, Mayseder will lead the band through its waltzes and polkas. The ceiling, too, so newly painted that I can smell it, is as sky blue as always. I picture the exact spot where we first rehearsed the first quartet of Opus 59.

Below me an array of guests, having been greeted by Count Rasumovsky, begin to occupy the walls; the older ladies, as always, keen to find and keep a chair. Across the wide, polished floor goes Princess Bagration, turning this way and that like a plump mechanical doll; around her the ladies' daughters like sugar confections, ready to dance and float, and then to melt back at night into their snowy beds. Soon the chairs have all been taken, and groups of nobles in uniform, black or white or blue, occupy the floor. And now, with scarcely a pause, come the guests of honour: first Metternich and Talleyrand, walking arm in arm; after them, escorted by the Count, our Emperor and the Tsar. The Empress and the Tsarina have declined their invitations.

I have not seen the Tsar – Alexander the First – quite so close before. Here, as at *Fidelio*, all eyes are turned on him, in his dazzling white uniform piped with gold, the silver star on his breast, and the halo of golden hair standing around his face. Yet, to me at least, the Count, who is a head taller, also looks magnificent now – wisely dressed in a plain coat of royal blue. His long face is grave, his bearing stiffly erect.

Metternich's wife stands nervously by, and I guess that she has been chosen to open the ball. I look towards my friends, the musicians, poised in the distance, beneath the new wooden extension, only waiting now for a signal from the Count.

Suddenly, right below me, there comes in a small green creature whose bald head looks from above like the stopper of a chemist's bottle. It is Peter Andreyich, dressed in a green uniform of new cloth, but absurd and ancient cut, on which some tarnished decorations appear to have settled like moths. Metternich steps from the Emperor's side and points the old man out to the Tsar, who glances in turn at Rasumovsky. Peter Andreyich goes down on one knee, his head almost touching the floor until, with gracious instinct, the Tsar holds out his gleaming hand. Peter Andreyich kisses it and staggers to his feet, and just for one second the whole room trembles with suppressed laughter, which of course he does not hear, as he turns and leaves. At last the band strikes up a waltz, under which I can see the rip-tide of gossip swirl. The couples wheel about, turning like the hundred cogs of some huge clock. Captain Ramballe, without his pelisse, is standing on his own, and I think to myself that surely, after all, tonight will pass away, leaving Rasumovsky able to retire from public life. The gossip will turn to someone else, providing he and Sophie remain discreet. The officers of the Tsar's guard, huge men also dressed in white, have taken off their swords to dance. Feeling tired of watching the dancers I look towards the orchestra, each of whom for this occasion is wearing our red livery. They are all old friends. Some, whose faces are hidden by the low roof of the extension, I pick out by their fingering. Hans is down there too, playing viola next to his father. Once more I watch his radiant limbs, the honey-gold of his instrument, the running flame of his hair. I see his future as a Viennese musician: one of those who mostly get by. Perhaps he will marry, or else be content with a friend or two, and a little shared place near the Bastion. He will dine at the Schwan and grow just a little stout.

Two hours of the ball have already slipped away and it is nearly supper-time. For the last hour the Tsar has not danced. He sits to one side with the Emperor, who has not danced at all. I slip back down to the Canova room, thinking to take a cold pie, when it suddenly occurs to me that I must go to the library and find the scores which were left there after our rehearsal. There is no Sophie, nor any Natalie now, to take them into the ballroom.

From the hall I glimpse a mighty sea of carriages and horses, waiting in the frozen dark. I walk down the corridor, hearing the strains of another waltz ahead of me. In the door of the store-room stands Karl. I think I hear the sound of a hammer before he slams the door in my face, but there is no time to think about him. I open the door of the library, and find myself confronted by Prince Metternich, Talleyrand, and the Russian with yellow teeth, whom I have seen in many salons these past few months. As I have guessed, our scores are still on the stands: the same scores, in Beethoven's hand, from which we have always played. The three diplomatists are sitting around the fire. Thinking how close Sophie is I almost wince as I bow to them and cross the room.

'Ugh! He is fat!' says the Russian, in French. 'Thank heavens the Tsar is not staying for supper, or this chamber music.'

'You see,' replies Metternich, laughing, 'how these musicians are pampered.'

Talleyrand nods by the fire, stretching out his narrow legs. Then, somehow, he gives me a little wink.

'You had best stay here,' he says, as I turn around and hear the sudden tide of feet. The dancing has ended, and through the door we see the Tsar and Emperor pass right by, followed by a swirl of dresses and uniforms. I hear the Count directing his other guests to the dining-room while he escorts the departing monarchs to the entrance, and I wonder will he think, or dare to absent himself, to go up to his study and spend ten precious minutes with Sophie?

In the ballroom a few guests linger. Hans, Weiss, Mayseder and Linke are waiting under the glass roof, and with them, to my surprise, Dorothy Ertmann and Therese. The Major, of course, is present too. I hand round the scores – and then I see the piano. Only then do I understand that this final concert will not be solely, as I had assumed, Opus 59, number 3 (and then, maybe, some impromptu dances), but that it will begin with a violin sonata. The Count, without consulting me, has decided to flaunt his newest wares. I look at young 'Leonore' dressed in her bright red silk, and pray he has chosen sonata number six or ten.

The Count, looking as calm as ever, has returned from supper alongside the Archduke Rudolph, whose bald head nods contentedly. He is Beethoven's pupil and patron, and there has never been any malice between him and the Count. There is no malice, in fact, between the Archduke and anyone. They seat themselves in the front row, where they are now joined by Metternich and Talleyrand. Kinsky, Lobkowitz, and a few more of our music-loving nobility arrive, along with the Dukes and Electors of half a dozen German states. The King of Prussia has either gone to bed or was never here. After them come in, again, elderly ladies beside pale young virgins in silk; diplomats with their wives; officers and glorious women, among whom I pick out both Princess Bagration and Countess Wilhemine de Sagan.

Standing against the wall I look up at the glass roof, which is now covered in moisture, and see the blurred image of a thousand stars. There are some whispers scattered amongst the polite applause as 'Leonore' steps forward; and just at this moment a small hot spark from the flue beside me lands like an insect on my neck. I feel a pulse of warm air. The Count is watching intently as Madame Ertmann plays the first notes and

Therese raises her bow. She plays like a statue coming to life; and often as I have heard it, and played it myself, the music sends a shiver down my spine. It is sonata number seven, the most dramatic of all.

Suddenly I hear a cracking which makes me think of fire; but then I can tell it is only the sound of heels on the polished floor. I look around for Peter Andreyich. No, he has not come in, and now the noise becomes louder and more rhythmical.

Three of the Tsar's guard, obviously drunk, have appeared from nowhere. One, the largest, with huge moustaches, squats down and kicks out his legs, his sabre bumping on the floor. His comrades stamp in time, treating Beethoven's jagged chords as if they were a Cossack dance. Rasumovsky darts from his place. I think he will beat them out of the room, but he merely glares at them until they shrink back against the opposite wall.

Beside me Weiss is trembling. He too glares at the Russians, and I put my arm on his shoulders to steady him. It has been a dangerous moment, but it has passed, and it occurs to me that Beethoven would have found the Cossacks amusing. Therese and Madame Ertmann, who have noticed nothing, glide on to the finale and rapturous applause. At the back the Major stands up and shouts bravo. Another small bright spark drops on Hans beside me, but in one quick movement I snuff it out of his hair. He looks down at me and smiles, wishing me good luck.

Quickly, then, the four of us sit down to play for the final time: Linke, Weiss, Mayseder, myself. Count Rasumovsky's eyes are on us as never before. I see Karl handing the Russians champagne, see Bilibin yawning, and then we play the opening dissonance, and I forget the audience. In my mind we are playing for Count Rasumovsky alone; and, although I don't look at him, I can sense that he, as always, is trying to comprehend this music which bears his name. In the end it is we who should be grateful that in this enterprise we have been included, and have spent so many hours with these quartets, which we too are still trying to understand. There will be some, at least, in this audience, who apprehend something of our struggles, though to most of them it will mean nothing at all. There is none, I think, who would have listened to it better than Princess Lichnowsky.

We are in the Andante. Linke, as ever, plucks the bass string with a grim, sensual twist. The minuet – we're almost home. Here Mayseder excels. And now Weiss leads off the Fuga: but suddenly he is no longer there. After a moment we realise that we have no viola, and our bows stop as one. It is impossible, but Weiss has disappeared.

Then I look across to the corner and see his fairish hair, and then his small, red frame thrusting between those three Russian officers. Before they have time to react he pulls Therese from among them, thrusts the glass door open, and they are gone. Linke and Mayseder are still looking into space. The audience wait, puzzled; luckily we and the platform have obscured their view, and someone has closed the door again. Opposite me Hans has picked up his father's viola. Behind him the Russians are talking drunkenly among themselves and pointing towards the door, but Hans nods to us and leads off the fuga again, jerking myself, Mayseder and Linke to respond. Someone at the back applauds. So we play, as we must do – faster, faster, faster. The Russians make for the door; and now I see Ramballe, his hand on his sabre, step in front of the Russians, who draw their weapons. He opens the door and steps outside, and there is the clash of metal on metal. Still we play, we cannot stop. The audience gasps, but no-one moves. They can see little of the figures beyond the door, in the space between the extension and Weiss's little cottage. So time stands still until we reach the final chord. As we do so Ramballe silently falls to the ground and the Russians leap over his body and into the night.

We receive a few stray hand-claps as the guests, as one, make for the front door in silence. A cold blast of air from outside ushers them on their way. Archduke Rudolph calls out 'Splendid!' while Talleyrand pauses to shake his head, and then they too are gone. We hear the clamour of people in the corridor, calling for their cloaks and furs, almost as if nothing had happened. And then we musicians, too, melt away from the French Captain, who lies outside bleeding and dead.

***

Once we have made our way upstairs Hans puts down his father's viola, next to his own Guarneri, with more than special care: then he lies down on the bed. I suppose I'm proud of him: he did it for his father's sake. Now he cannot take any more. I cover him and stroke his hair and he is soon asleep. I wish that I could sleep. I wish we had gone back to my house, but something made me come up here: perhaps it was the simple fact that all the others left. After all, the palace has been hospitable, and exciting. Now there is so much mischief afoot, I am more inclined to stay. I remember the Count so often mocking Metternich's fellow, Karl, and perhaps he was wrong; but I am glad that he mocked him. He will dismiss him, after that prank; but no doubt he has already left. What else? I cannot think. Some of the servants are loyal. Will anything be said? Will they put Ramballe in the stables with Natalie, a French man and woman together? The Count remained behind with him, but I am sure he was dead. Weiss and Therese escaped – I am almost certain of that. Everything happened so fast that no-one will be sure it took place.

I go to the window and look out into the night, where the stars are scattered like a thousand diamonds. The moon has shifted position behind the slowly-growing web of frost on the window-pane. The bare apple-trees cast shadows. Further away, beyond a low wall, the frozen canal is pimpled with light.

Looking up again I notice the lighted first floor window of the Brentano-Birkenstock house, and think I see the shapes of people inside. I put another blanket over Hans and carefully move the telescope into place. I open the window quietly and then sit down on the chair to look.

There are six people altogether. First I see Beethoven, with Antonie and Franz Brentano. They are all three holding hands. I have to turn my spyglass to pick out the other three, who are standing a little apart. They are Weiss, Therese, and Princess Lichnowsky. Therese is wrapped in a shawl. I try to recall if she had her violin in her hand, when she fled, but I cannot remember.

They give me the impression of a living tableau, for all six are looking out intently at the palace, and suddenly I smell the smoke…smoke, and the crackle of flame. I wonder if I am dreaming all of this until, incontrovertible, a sudden cloud of black smoke drifts across my gaze.

I force myself to shake Hans hard. He sleeps the careless sleep of youth. Go, I tell him, break the partitions, rouse the maids, for we are on fire! Go – shout – raise the alarm up here. I will rouse the floor below. We are on fire!

Downstairs the secretaries are already awake and fleeing. I wait for Hans on the landing. It is most horrible, waiting, but I can tell he is doing well. Someone is ringing a bell, and all the young men and maids, some with blankets round their shoulders, some carrying their clothes and boots, come rushing down the stairs. At last he comes. We go together. As we descend the final red steps I see, along the corridor leading to the ballroom, a roaring dragon of smoke and flame. It seems to pause and crouch for a moment. I do not wait to see more.

Outside in the street we stand with the rest and shiver and watch. The building appears strangely tranquil, as if it were no more than a haystack, as if the wisps and whorls of smoke squeezing out of it here and there were really no more than a summer morning's mist. Then there's a sudden glow of orange and then, with a terrible crash, a window bursts and flames lick out. It is the library. Now, with hardly a pause, the fire moves upwards and sideways until, on the other side, the skylight of the Canova room crashes onto the heads of the statues. We all move backwards, away from the heat. Some men have arrived with buckets, but it's far too late. Above us now the pall of smoke has almost obscured the moon. Clutching my fiddle against my chest I look around.

I can see all the secretaries, the other senior staff and, in dressing gowns, Monsieur and Madame Bigot. When they came back, like many others, simply to observe the Congress, the Count insisted on taking them in. All the cooks and men and maids, and the porter, seem to be here. Hans is here and I am here. I pray that those I cannot see will be found alive.

Standing behind us I notice a stranger. A tall man, he alone is dressed for the cold, in a dark greatcoat with a woollen scarf over his chin, and a heavy, broad-brimmed hat. He keeps his face in shadow, turning aside if a flame leaps up, for still the palace burns and burns. In spite of his wrappings he seems like a statue – a coil of energy, frozen – like something I once saw, a copy, by Michelangelo. I believe it is Karl, the author of who knows what mischief and I believe that this horror has something to do with him. Or perhaps he is here to take the news to Metternich. I turn and step towards him, angrily.

I am in front of him now, less than a yard away, and find myself looking straight into the eyes of the Count. I look again, and bow my head. Eventually he lifts his hand and pulls the scarf away from his mouth. His face is utter ruin. Although he has taken me in he is looking past me, at the inferno, as if, at any moment, he might hurl himself at it; but there is nothing he can do.

'Ah,' he says, at last, 'my dear fellow. You played it well. But what a night! I have been walking, to clear my head, and – you see what has happened.'

Mechthilt has also heard of the fire, and has been sobbing with fear. As day dawns our neighbours gather to tell us the latest news. The palace has collapsed. Someone had the presence of mind to let out the horses and knock down the stables, stopping the fire from spreading that way. They found the dead French maid in there. There is a rumour that someone else was killed: some poor soul who was caught in the very heart of the blaze. Some say a foreign serving-woman – from Prussia, or maybe from Poland. Some say another, a very old man, a Russian they think, but not well-known. Some say there were two, or three.

Two days later the fire is old news. Rumour from Congress says the Tsar is adamant in his demands. Naturally he has accepted Prince Rasumovsky's resignation. Rumour has it that we, the French, and even the British, have sworn to oppose, even by force, Russia's claim to Poland. After all that we have suffered there might be another war. Apparently, though, the Tsar has had time not only to thank Rasumovsky for his serviccs, but to remark that he greatly approves his patronage of music here. Music belongs to all nations. He was deeply moved by the opera he attended. By Beethoven, was it not? The Empress Elizaveta is also very much taken with this German music: symphonies, and holy things.

***

The world goes on: there will even be one more battle with Napoleon, after his escape from Elba, but far away from us. After each occupation by foreign powers, right back to the Turks, no doubt, Vienna has carried on in its mainly tolerant way. So it does after the Congress – except that Countess Erdody is banished. Linke goes with her to Hungary, but he cannot stay away for ever. Weiss and Mayseder also depart – one to Breslau, one to Paris – but they, too, will return. Rasumovsky becomes a recluse (although, in old age, he marries again), Princess Lichnowsky dies of a chill, and Metternich reigns supreme – but that fellow Karl drops out of sight. Hans and Therese get married. They live with Anna Linke, and are poor but happy. Hans plays clarinet in the Karnthenor orchestra.

I still have much work, as Beethoven does, and like him I am rarely satisfied. One day I will go to Russia. I need the money. Meanwhile I have new colleagues around me, new quartet players to teach, but I am always glad to make time for Weiss, Mayseder, or Linke; and, whenever two of us meet, we are bound to remember Sophie.

Endnote

In concert with my characters, I urgently recommend Beethoven's string quartets! While I have had some irreverent fun, and drawn some patterns to create a little distance, I have also tried to create an impression of life for musicians and composers in Vienna in 1809-14, at a time when they were just beginning to escape the servant class. Many, if not quite all, of my musicians and other characters derive from people mentioned in Alexander Wheelock Thayer's biography of *Beethoven*. This I gradually supplemented by reading a variety of social and political histories of Europe, memoirs and biographies, and, of course, by internet searches. I learned that five-plate stoves were being adopted by the Austrian middle-classes, Olympe de Gouge was an early French feminist, and Metternich really did favour canary yellow. Alistair Horne's military and political history *How Far from Austerlitz?* gave me a useful overview, and Tolstoy's *War and Peace* gave me some ideas. Readers who want more Beethoven than I have given them may enjoy John Suchet's fictional account of the whole life in *The Last Master*. Should you have enjoyed this book please do get in touch via markpaffard@gmail.com

Mark Paffard, 2019.

*

Printed in Poland
by Amazon Fulfillment
Poland Sp. z o.o., Wrocław